TRAIL OF TERROR

The Trailsman had no trouble tracking the Utes through the forest. The first hint of trouble came when he found them—one by one.

The first had his face smashed to a pulp. The second lay with his arm ripped from his body, while his horse lay nearby with a snapped neck. Next Skye found a torn-off redskin head, its eyes bulging in hideous fear.

Up ahead Skye heard sounds of conflict. He saw the remaining Indians struggling against a creature twice as big as they. Skye started shooting, trying not to hit the Utes. At the second shot, the nightmare being stiffened, then wheeled and melted into the vegetation, vanishing without a trace.

By the time Skye reached the Ute chief, White Eagle, the tall warrior had only minutes to live. Skye stooped to look at him, the spurting blood from the slashed copper-colored chest soaking the Trailsman's boots.

"Flee," the Indian told him. "Save yourself."

Easier said than done . . .

THE
TRAILSMAN

184

ROCKY MOUNTAIN NIGHTMARE

by

Jon Sharpe

A SIGNET BOOK

SIGNET
Published by the Penguin Group
Penguin Books USA Inc., 375 Hudson Street,
New York, New York 10014, U.S.A.
Penguin Books Ltd, 27 Wrights Lane,
London W8 5TZ, England
Penguin Books Australia Ltd, Ringwood,
Victoria, Australia
Penguin Books Canada Ltd, 10 Alcorn Avenue,
Toronto, Ontario, Canada M4V 3B2
Penguin Books (N.Z.) Ltd, 182–190 Wairau Road,
Auckland 10, New Zealand

Penguin Books Ltd, Registered Offices:
Harmondsworth, Middlesex, England

First published by Signet, an imprint of Dutton Signet,
a division of Penguin Books USA Inc.

First Printing, April, 1997
10 9 8 7 6 5 4 3 2 1

The Trailsman

Beginnings . . . they bend the tree and they mark the man. Skye Fargo was born when he was eighteen. Terror was his midwife, vengeance his first cry. Killing spawned Skye Fargo, ruthless, cold-blooded murder. Out of the acrid smoke of gunpowder still hanging in the air, he rose, cried out a promise never forgotten.

The Trailsman they began to call him all across the West: searcher, scout, hunter, the man who could see where others only looked, his skills for hire but not his soul, the man who lived each day to the fullest, yet trailed each tomorrow. Skye Fargo, the Trailsman, and the seeker who could take the wildness of a land and the wanting of a woman and make them his own.

1861, high up in the Rockies—
where if a man wasn't careful, all that thin air
might have him seeing things . . .

1

The raging snowstorm struck without warning.

For the better part of an hour Skye Fargo had been toiling up a steep slope choked with firs and deadfalls. The few glimpses he caught of the sky showed patches of bright blue and fluffy clouds. He had no inkling of the terrible tantrum fickle Nature was about to throw.

Then the big man in buckskins rode out of the trees onto a barren jagged spine high atop the towering Rocky Mountains. He reined up so his weary Ovaro could rest.

Shifting in the saddle, Fargo caught a blast of frigid air full in the face. Squinting his lake-blue eyes, he was startled to see a massive bank of roiling gray clouds sweeping in from the west. Already the storm front was on the other side of the valley he had just crossed. It would be on him in minutes.

Swearing luridly, the Trailsman applied his spurs. The pinto stallion, sensing his unease, trotted along the spine to where a narrow game trail wound down from the lofty heights.

Fargo's lips tightened. Made by mountain sheep, mule deer, elk, and bear, the trail was no wider than his broad shoulders. Worse, in many places it was flanked by sheer cliffs. A single misstep would spell doom.

Yet Fargo had no choice but to descend and seek cover. The temperature was dropping rapidly. Caught in the open, he would be battered by the merciless elements.

There was no telling how many men had lost their lives

to the high country's notoriously fickle weather. Scores, maybe. Men who, like Fargo, were caught flat-footed by raging storms that swept out of nowhere to engulf them in blinding sheets of snow and ice.

Fargo kneed the Ovaro down the trail. Its hooves sent small stones clattering over a precipice. Leaning out, Fargo saw the bottom, strewn with boulders, over a thousand feet below. He shuddered to think of the consequences should he follow those stones down.

Howling like a banshee, the wind grew stronger by the moment. It buffeted Fargo and the pinto, forcing him to pull his hat down around his ears and hunch his shoulders against the gale. A few flakes of snow danced in the air like tiny white fireflies. They were harbingers of the swarm to come.

Rounding a bend, Fargo rose in the stirrups to scan the mountainside. Another valley beckoned far, far below. But it would take as long to reach it as it had taken to climb to the ridge. By then the full force of the snowstorm would be unleashed.

The trail wound haphazardly toward a spur of rock that cut off Fargo's view of whatever lay beyond. A rush of icy wind brought goose bumps to his flesh. More and more flakes cavorted wildly in the rarefied atmosphere, almost as if they were taunting him. A few landed on his neck and hands, melting instantly, their cold touch a promise of the icy death that would be his if he was not careful.

Fargo came to the rock spur. As he went around it, the storm hit with all the elemental fury of an airborne tidal wave. Shrieking wind pummeled the peaks. A thick white blanket engulfed him. It became so cold that he could see puffs of his breath.

All was not lost, though. In the few seconds before the storm swallowed him whole, Fargo spotted a broad table-land several hundred feet lower. It had to be half a mile wide. Pines offered a safe haven, if only he could reach them.

Fargo abruptly stiffened, doubting his sanity. In the center of the tableland reared what appeared to be an immense man-made structure. He blinked against the driving snow, raising a hand to shield his eyes for a better look.

The raging white sheet closed around him like a glove. Fargo could not see his palm at arm's length, let alone the tableland. He shook his head, certain his eyes had deceived him. By his best reckoning he was sixty or seventy miles west of Denver, deep in the heart of the Rockies. Other than a few scattered mining camps, the region was uninhabited.

Except for roving bands of marauding Utes, of course.

Fargo forged on, holding the stallion to a slow walk, stopping often to bend down. The trail had narrowed. On his left loomed a rock wall; on his right the sheer drop-off. He had counted at least two more bends before he reached the tableland, but he could not be sure of exactly where they were.

It was a nightmare, that descent. What should have taken ten minutes took over an hour. Twice the Ovaro slipped, and each time Fargo's heart leaped into his throat as he felt the pinto start to go over the side. In each instance it regained its footing, snorting and quivering with fright.

All the while, the storm roared and fumed around them, lashing them with snow and wind and cold. Since it was only early fall, Fargo had not brought a coat along. Until the storm appeared, the weather had been extremely mild. So much so, that at night Fargo had lain under the sparkling stars with no blanket to cover him.

Now Fargo wished that he could take the time to unfasten his bedroll and wrap himself in a blanket or two. He was freezing. His buckskins were half-soaked, his skin a sheen of ice. His teeth took to chattering. Clamping them tight, he hunched forward to ward off the driving wind. It did no good.

Just when Fargo's nerves were frayed to the breaking point, the stallion nickered and bobbed its head. The rock wall to the left of them was gone. Cautiously, Fargo dismounted, to discover that they had finally reached the tableland.

Leading the pinto, Fargo trudged toward a dim dark wall that had to be the forest. He clasped his arms to his chest for added warmth. The wind screamed shrilly, as if outraged that he would soon be safe.

Suddenly Fargo halted. Cocking his head, he listened intently. It had to be his imagination, because the scream that he was hearing sounded as if it issued from an inhuman throat. He shook his head, amused by his foolishness. No animals would be out in such foul weather. Grizzlies, mountain lions, and wolves would all be lying low until the worst was past—just as he should be doing.

Tramping on through the snow that was six inches deep and growing deeper by the minute, Fargo was overjoyed when somber ranks of pines loomed in front of him. Relieved, he entered the woodland. He paused to remove his hat and slap snow from his shoulders.

Here the worst of the tempest was blunted. The snow still fell thickly, but he could see for a dozen feet or so. And the wind was quieter, its icy bite no more than an annoying sting.

Smiling, Fargo put his hat back on, then froze in the act of adjusting the brim. From out of the pines on his left rose the same piercing scream he had heard earlier. This time there could be no doubt that it was not the wind. It was a living creature, but its scream was unlike any Fargo had ever heard.

Automatically, Fargo's right hand dropped to the butt of his Colt. He glanced at the Ovaro, which stood with ears pricked and nostrils flaring, staring into the dense growth that surrounded them. Something was definitely out there. *But what?*

Fargo was not superstitious by nature. Many Indian tribes believed the wilds were home to all sorts of spirits and unearthly creatures, but he had never been one to believe in something unless he saw it with his own eyes.

His scalp prickling, Fargo went on. He made no sound that could be heard above the wind, but the dull thud of the stallion's hooves were bound to attract whatever was out there. And they did.

Without warning, a shape materialized at the limits of Fargo's vision. Dumbfounded, he stopped.

A tall, thin figure swayed on two spindly legs, its features blurred by the whipping white curtain. Lean arms lifted as if it were about to spring, and from its lips burst that horrid scream, only now the scream held a new note, a note of bloodthirsty rage.

Fargo's Colt leaped clear. His thumb curled the hammer back. Just as his finger began to caress the trigger, the eerie apparition vanished. He glanced to either side, thinking that it might circle and come at him from a different direction. Tense minutes passed, but the creature did not reappear.

Warily, Fargo hiked deeper into the forest. Above and around him the trees were being whipped ferociously. Limbs bent and creaked. Many snapped and cracked. It was impossible to pinpoint the screaming devil that he was sure stalked him.

A thicket materialized. Rather than go around, Fargo plowed into the cover, which rose as high as his chest. Whatever was out there would not be able to get at him, he thought. But he was wrong.

He found out when the stallion whinnied and shied. A feral snarl explained why. Claws raked Fargo's left leg. Instinctively, he jumped to the right.

A dim bulk was crouched at the base of a bush. It howled like a demented wolf, slashing fiercely at the pinto, which lurched backward just as Fargo was going to fire.

Yanked off balance, it was all Fargo could do to hold onto the reins. The figure flowed back into the gloom that had spawned it as Fargo fought to keep the pinto from fleeing in panic.

Another savage screech proved too much for the Ovaro. Nickering and bucking, it tore loose and bolted. The crash of undergrowth was the only way Fargo had of marking its flight.

He gave chase. To be stranded afoot in the wilderness was a death warrant for most. For a frontiersman of his caliber, for someone who had lived among Indians and knew how to live off the land as well as they did, it would not be as bad. But he would be lucky to reach Denver alive.

Heedless of the lurker in the storm, Fargo ran as fast as the terrain allowed. He weaved among trunks. He vaulted logs. He barreled through tracts of heavy brush. In his ears hissed the wind. The snow had tapered, though not by much.

A boulder the size of a log cabin barred his path, and Fargo raced on around. Out of the corner of his right eye he saw a shadow detach itself and surge toward him. Before he could halt or turn, the thing attacked.

A heavy body slammed into Fargo's back. The jarring impact knocked him to his hands and knees. Claws seared into his neck. He twisted, then suddenly realized that the claws were not really claws at all. He could feel the pressure of fingers and thumbs gouging into his flesh.

The claws were fingernails! Nails as long as the talons of birds of prey, as sharp as the fangs of cougars.

Fargo wrenched around, or tried to, but the figure clung to him with ghoulish strength. The nails dug deeper, drawing blood that froze almost as quickly as it oozed out. He flailed his elbows back and in, connecting with iron ribs. It elicited a screech of raw fury, but the wraith did not let go.

Frantically, Fargo threw himself from side to side. His beastly assailant snarled and those awful fingers dug deeper. Then, by chance more than by design, Fargo collided with a tree. Pivoting, he slammed his attacker against the bole, again and again.

The fourth time was the charm. Yowling like a rabid coyote, the apparition released him. Fargo spun, leveling the Colt. But as he brought the pistol up, the figure whirled and leaped like a two-legged bobcat. Steel-spring muscles carried it into undergrowth eight feet away.

Panting from his exertion, stung and sore and bleeding, Fargo ran to the same spot. The man was gone. He turned every which way, seeking some sign, but the snow and the vegetation conspired to thwart him.

A baffled oath burst from the Trailsman's lips. His trigger finger literally itched to stroke the trigger. He dashed a few yards into the trees, drawing up short when the futility of what he was trying to do impressed itself.

Backing to the boulder, Fargo resumed his search for the Ovaro. During the brief struggle he had been unable to tell if his attacker was white or red. Why the man wanted to kill him, he had no idea. He suspected that the mysterious stalker was somewhere nearby, waiting for an opportunity to try again.

How far Fargo ran, he could not say—maybe two hundred yards. The wind slackened, but the snow thickened, severely limiting visibility.

Fargo stopped to catch his breath. The moment he did, a vague, ghastly specter rushed shrieking from the pines, ramming into him with frightening speed. Bowled over, his arms pinned against his body, Fargo felt teeth rake his neck. The wild man was striving to tear open his jugular!

Horror goaded Fargo into twisting and thrashing like a madman. His left arm broke free. He rained punches on the figure's head, but he might as well have been striking the ground. The growling, snapping figure held on.

They must have rolled over the brink of a knoll, because the next thing Fargo knew, they tumbled down a short slope littered with sharp rocks. At the bottom a boulder brought them to a stop.

For once, luck worked in Fargo's favor. The wild man bore the brunt. Screeching like a stricken catamount, the man shoved upright and fled, favoring his left leg. Fargo rose to his knees and took a hasty bead, but not quite hasty

15

enough. Once again the apparition disappeared before he could fire.

Fargo's hat had fallen off. Groping about, he found it and smacked it against his leg to shed snow. Circling the boulder, he moved off in a crouch. He was actually glad when the storm worsened. Every bit of extra cover helped.

His right boot bumped something. Stooping lower, he figured to find a large rock or a limb. Instead, his probing fingers roved over the stump of a sapling. The grooved surface told him that the tree had been chopped down, not blown over.

Indians would rather gather fallen branches than chop wood. They made their fires so small that an armful lasted all night.

Odds were, then, that whoever cut down the sapling had been white. Perhaps a prospector had staked a claim in the area, or an old trapper had a cabin nearby. Neither would explain the unprovoked attack.

Mystified, Fargo stalked on, always on the alert. He had covered a quarter of a mile when the wind tapered to a low moan and the snow dwindled to steady but widely spaced flakes. It was either a lull in the storm, or it was smaller in size and scope than he had reckoned.

Fargo could distinguish individual trees and other landmarks. He hoped his attacker would come after him now, when he could see well enough to get off a clear shot, but the wild man had apparently given up. It was tempting to start a fire and rest a spell, but he pushed on after the Ovaro.

Drifting snow had erased whatever tracks the stallion made. Fargo constantly looked for sign, to no avail. A clearing spread out before him. There he paused, debating whether to cut straight across and expose himself to the phantom.

It was then that a new sound fluttered through the woodland, a sound that shocked Fargo as much as the screams had earlier. He tossed his head, but he still heard it. He slapped his ear, but it was working just fine. Lastly, he pinched himself to verify it was not a dream. He was wide awake.

Why, then, did he hear the musical lilt of a woman's throaty voice, humming gaily as if she did not have a single care in the world? It couldn't be, he told himself. The nearest women were in mining camps twenty to thirty miles east of where he was.

The humming grew louder. Through the trees across the clearing a human form flitted. Fargo could not quite believe his eyes. It was a woman, sure enough, dressed in clothes as white as the snow, skipping along as if she were taking a merry stroll through a city park. In her right hand she swung something large back and forth.

Totally bewildered, Fargo veered to intercept her. There was a chance she had seen the Ovaro. Then, too, he needed to warn her about the wild man. His footfalls were muffled by the heavy snow, so he was almost on top of her before she sensed another presence and turned.

Fargo stopped, smiling to demonstrate that he was friendly. "Don't be afraid," he said. It did not help.

The woman took one look at him and the revolver he clasped, and lit out of there as if her heels were on fire. She did not cry out or scream, though, which in itself was odd.

"Wait!" Fargo hollered, to no avail. She fled like a frightened doe, threading through the trees with a skill that hinted at long experience in the wild. He sped after her, tantalized by the glimpse he'd had of wavy raven hair framed by an ermine hood and an alluring face as milky and smooth as the finest cream.

When the woman had turned, Fargo recognized the object she held. Like the wild man and the woman herself, it was out of place, bizarre. The sight of it was almost enough to convince him that the woman must be a figment of his overworked imagination.

Here he was, in the middle of nowhere with a snowstorm fading rapidly around him, and what should he stumble on but a beautiful woman in a white fur coat, traipsing through the forest *with a picnic basket* in her hand!

"Wait!" Fargo called again, struggling to keep the vision of loveliness in view. Her white coat blended so perfectly into the white background that if not for the brown basket, she would have been invisible. Several times she cast petrified glances over her slender shoulder.

"I won't hurt you!" Fargo called out. He should have saved his breath. She kept on fleeing, a pale ghost among ghostly trees, leaving tracks that were uncommonly shallow, almost as if she spurned the ground in her flight.

The snowfall had abated even more. In the storm's wake the mountains had been transformed into a pristine hoary wonderland. A thick white shroud covered everything. It layered branches in frosty white. It mantled brush in chalky hues. Logs were white bumps on the forest floor. Boulders had dandruff.

It occurred to Fargo that the woman was gradually looping her way back to the general area where he had spotted her. The insight spurred him into cutting through a grassy belt to head her off. She did not notice. Intent on eluding him, she did not awaken to his ploy until he crashed through high weeds beside her and grasped her wrist.

"No!" the woman wailed, jerking and tugging in a frenzy. "Let go of me!"

"I only want to warn you—," Fargo said, but got no further. In desperation the woman swung the picnic basket at his head. He ducked a shade slow. It clipped him on the temple hard enough to buckle his legs. Pain seared his skull and his vision spun.

The woman tore loose. A thud heralded her flight. Fargo, shaking his head to clear it, pushed to his feet just as a thicket closed around her fur-bundled form. He took a faltering stride, intending to chase her however far it took to bring her to bay, when something snagged his right foot, trapping him. He went to one knee.

Assuming that a log or boulder was to blame, Fargo

began to rise once more. He changed his mind when he discovered that the object he had fallen over was her picnic basket. She had flung it aside so she would not be burdened by the extra weight.

Fargo holstered his pistol. Enough was enough. The woman had made it plain that she wanted nothing to do with him. So be it. He'd go find the stallion and continue his trek eastward.

First, though, Fargo opened the basket, not knowing what to expect. But what else would a picnic basket contain? Food galore had been packed to the brim. Salted strips of beef, fragrant cheeses, canned goods, crackers and more, all had been neatly arranged to make the most of the limited space.

His mouth watered, his stomach rumbled. Two days had gone by since he ate last, and he was famished. Fargo scanned the woods, but saw no trace of the woman. She might object to his helping himself, but after what she had done, he felt that he deserved to. After all, he had only been trying to warn her about the man who tried to kill him a while ago. She had no call to turn on him as she had done.

The beef proved too tantalizing to resist. Fargo bit off a sizable chunk, smacking his lips at the delicious flavor. A few mouthfuls convinced him that it was the tastiest, juiciest jerky he had ever eaten, and that said a lot.

Standing, Fargo walked eastward, chewing lustily. Clouds rolled by overhead, but the snow had about ended, and the wind had died. No one could sneak up on him any longer. He would be safe so long as he stuck to open ground.

His hunger merely whetted, Fargo regarded the assortment of cheeses with interest. It would serve the woman right, he reflected, if he finished off every last morsel. Plucking out a yellowish-green wedge that stank to high heaven, he bit half off. It tasted a lot better than it smelled. A brown wedge had a spicy taste. A third was soft and mushy.

The forest had thinned to scattered stands of pines. The woman was nowhere to be seen, but Fargo had a hunch that she was close by, spying on him.

Cramming salted crackers into his mouth, the big man made for a rise that overlooked the eastern half of the tableland. The food had made him thirsty enough to drain a river. So he was delighted when he lifted a packet of meat and found a full whiskey bottle lying on its side.

Beaming, Fargo came to the top of the rise and set the basket down. Whoever that woman had been, she knew the way to a man's heart! Eagerly, he opened the heaven-sent gift. Straightening, he tipped the whiskey to his mouth, but never swallowed. For as his gaze roved beyond the rise, he went rigid with amazement and questioned his sanity.

A stone's throw away reared the structure he had seen from afar. It had no business being there, yet it was undeniably real. As alien as the wild man and the woman in white, before him sprawled an enormous, brooding castle.

2

Skye Fargo had been bitten by the wanderlust bug when he was in his early teens. Ever since, he had spent his days roaming from one end of the country to the other. He had ventured north to Alaska, south into Mexico. Few men in his day and age had covered half as much territory.

In all that roaming, Fargo had seen many strange and wonderful sights: polar bears on ice floes, whales as large as steamboats, Indians who pierced their noses and ears and filed their teeth to sharp points, and so much more. He had seen buildings of all kinds, from stately French-style mansions in New Orleans to tall office buildings in cities back East to sprawling adobe haciendas in the Southwest.

But it was safe to say that the Trailsman had never laid eyes on any structure as strange and outlandish as the stone edifice that sat in the center of the snow-covered tableland like a great squat toad in hibernation.

No lights shone in any of the windows. No figures moved about on any of the ramparts. The castle appeared to be deserted, but instinct told Fargo otherwise. He swore that he could feel unseen eyes watching him, taking his measure.

The odor of the whiskey reminded him of the drink he had been about to take before shock rooted him in place. He took a long, healthy swig, relishing the burning warmth that spread down his throat and into his belly. Coughing, he took another swallow, studying the castle from under his hat brim.

The initial appearance of great size had been somewhat misleading. True, it was immense compared to, say, the average house in Denver. But he doubted that it was as big as the castles in Europe he had heard of.

It covered about an acre. Outer walls had not been erected, nor had its builder gone to the trouble of ringing it with a moat. Not that either were needed. The castle walls themselves were as high as tall trees and crowned by battlements. At each corner reared a turret. A small force could hold the place against a horde of red devils, if need be.

In the middle of the south wall stood a large metal gateway, or portcullis. It was closed. Through the bars Fargo caught sight of twin wooden double doors, likewise shut. A rutted excuse for a road wound eastward from the gate. The depth and number of the ruts were a clue as to how the massive stone blocks had been brought in.

Fargo debated whether to go down and see if anyone was home. He still had the Ovaro to find. Raising the whiskey bottle for a last drink, he detected movement at the rear corner of the castle. A recessed iron door, not apparent at first, had swung open. He had a fleeting glimpse of a white-clad figure darting inside. Then the door clanged shut.

So now he knew where the vision of loveliness in white had come from. Capping the whiskey, he thrust it into the basket and marched down the rise to stand in the shadow of a great wall.

The storm front had passed on by. Gradually, the sky to the west was clearing. Shafts of sunlight had broken through, dappling the ivory landscape with shimmering brilliance. An hour of daylight remained, no more.

Fargo walked to the gate, deposited the basket, and looked up in time to spy a head that ducked into one of the windows. Cupping his mouth, he shouted, "Have you seen any sign of a pinto stallion? It ran off in the storm."

The skulker refused to reply. Fargo pounded on the gate a few times, but that, too, brought no response. Shrugging his broad shoulders, he walked off.

Whoever lived there had a lot to learn about western ways. Hospitality was a byword on the frontier, where folks were friendly to strangers as a matter of course. Anyone who showed up at a ranch house toward supper time was always treated to a meal and a spot to bed down.

Fargo had taken a dozen steps when voices erupted in anger behind him. He glanced at the window. A man and a woman were arguing heatedly, their words muffled. He could not quite make out what they were saying. After listening a few moments, he went on. Whatever they were upset about was none of his business.

"Hold up there, mister! There's no need for you to be running off with night about to fall."

The speaker was a middle-aged man who had poked his tousled head out of the castle window. He smiled when Fargo looked up, then nodded at the portcullis. "My man-servant will open the gate for you. Please, wait until I get down there. I'll only be a minute."

Fargo hesitated. He'd rather go after the Ovaro. But the *hombre* seemed genuinely friendly, and a few minutes delay would not hurt. He tramped back to the heavy metal grill.

Within seconds the twin wooden doors creaked open. Since the man had mentioned a servant, Fargo imagined some sort of fancy butler would let him in. Instead, a huge, massive figure was framed by the curved jambs, a figure oddly misshapen and somehow sinister. Mired in deep shadow, the servant shuffled to one side, turning toward the Trailsman a single eye that glittered like the eyes of wolves in firelight.

Stiffening, Fargo's hand strayed to his Colt. The manservant gripped a thick rope with arms as wide as tree trunks and began to pull. The portcullis rattled upward, revealing that the vertical bars had wicked points at the bottom.

Making the rope fast, the servant lumbered out to regard Fargo much as a grizzly might regard an animal it was sizing up for a meal. It was a fitting analogy. The man had the bulk of a bear, his powerful frame rippling with corded muscle. But fate had played a cruel trick on him at birth.

Fargo had never seen anyone so misshapen. One barrel of a leg was inches shorter than the other, one crooked arm half a foot longer than its mate. The right shoulder slanted upward, the left angled down. The body itself was grossly deformed, as if cruel hands had twisted it at will when still in the womb.

Worst of all was the man's face. The right half was unmarred: a strong chin, a full cheek, a smooth brow, and that single glittering eye hinted at how handsome the man would have been if not for the foul jest life played on him. For the left half was a mockery of everything human. Mottled skin hung in folds like rings of melted wax. The jaw was slack, the mouth always open and dribbling spittle, the nose flared to twice its natural width, and the eye, if there was one, sunken in layers of loose skin that hung from a brow covered with bony knobs.

Inwardly, Fargo recoiled. Then he chided himself for being childish. The poor man could not help how he looked. And among the many lessons Fargo had learned in his travels was the truth of the old saw that appearances could be deceiving. Despite that coldly gleaming eye, the manservant might be as gentle as a lamb.

"Skye Fargo," Fargo introduced himself, offering his hand.

The hulking servant seemed surprised. Almost reluctantly he extended his right arm, his thick fingers gripping Fargo's for just a second. It was enough to hint at the latent power in those gnarled limbs, giving Fargo the impression that if the servant wanted to, the man could crush his fingers as if they were brittle twigs.

As the servant bent, Fargo noticed something else. High on the fellow's back was a hump as big as the picnic basket. The man was a hunchback.

"What's your name?" Fargo asked.

The manservant's mouth worked, but no sounds came out. He fidgeted uneasily and shifted to stare at the gate.

"Quite a place you've got here," Fargo said to be sociable. "It must have cost a fortune."

"More money than most men make in a lifetime."

It was not the hunchback who answered. Bustling through the entrance came the middle-aged man, a fur-lined cloak swirling about his rotund form. Receding brown hair, gray at the temples, bordered a moon face that split into a sincere smile of greeting. "Hello, stranger. I'm Jim Conover. I live here."

Conover made the last remark as if he were not entirely happy about the fact. They shook, and Fargo told who he was, adding, "I didn't mean to trespass on your property. To tell the truth, I had no idea anyone lived in these parts. I thought the nearest homesteads were around Georgetown."

"They are. But my wife insisted that we build our winter home way out here. Castle Conover, as we call it, was finished about a year ago."

Fargo could not help but note that the man did not take any particular pride in his unique home. "You haven't happened to have seen anything of a pinto in the past hour or so, have you?"

"Can't say that I have, but then I was in my study, reading during the storm, and only came out when I overheard the maids jabbering about a mountain man one of them had spotted." Conover faced the hunchback. "What about you, Quirinoc? You're always up on the ramparts. Have you seen Mr. Fargo's mount?"

The manservant shook his ponderous head.

"I'm afraid that Quirinoc can't talk," Conover revealed. "One of his previous employers cut out his tongue."

"What?" Fargo said, appalled.

"It happened over a decade ago, in France," Conover explained. "Long before he started working for my wife. She brought him with her to our country." Again, in his tone was a suggestion that he was not entirely pleased by his wife's decision.

The sun had dipped to the level of the treetops. Lengthening shadows spread from the forest toward the castle as if eager to devour it. With the approach of evening the temperature was dropping swiftly. By nightfall it would be below freezing.

"I'll be on my way, then," Fargo said. He was growing anxious about the Ovaro. Normally, the dependable stallion would have returned to him on its own. He feared that something had happened.

"Nonsense!" Jim Conover said. "I won't hear of it! Where could you find better shelter? You're more than welcome to spend the night with us."

At that moment a woman strolled through the gate. Emerald eyes fixed on Fargo and frankly lingered. "So it's true we have a visitor. Introduce me, James, if you would be so kind." She had a lilting accent, and wore a blue satin dress that outlined the sensual contours of her full figure. Luxuriant black hair cascaded over finely molded shoulders. Features as smooth as marble were chiseled in lines of classical beauty.

Fargo was sure it was the same woman he had bumped into in the woods. He was going to mention as much, but when he opened his mouth, she tensed, as if in dread. On an impulse he changed his mind and settled for saying, "I thought I was dreaming when I first saw this place."

"Skye Fargo, meet Arlette, the apple of my eye."

The beauty's ripe lips quirked downward. "Honestly, husband. Sometimes your quaint homespun customs can be quite annoying." She extended her hand. "I am Countess Arlette Leonie Mignon d'Arcy Conover, at your humble service."

"That handle of yours is quite a mouthful," Fargo said. Her palm was warm, and her fingers caressed him as she withdrew them.

Jim Conover sighed. "My wife is fond of pomp and ceremony, Mr. Fargo. It comes from being royalty, I reckon."

The countess clucked like an irate hen. "A true gentleman does not use the barbaric expression, 'I reckon.' How many time must I correct you? The next time we visit the Continent, I insist that your manners be impeccable."

Conover rolled his eyes heavenward. "Whatever you desire, my dear, I always aim to please." To Fargo, he said, "Wait here a moment while I fetch some horses. Maybe we can locate your pinto before dark." He hurried inside.

The countess rose on tiptoe to whisper something into the hunchback's ear. Quirinoc immediately lumbered into the castle on some errand.

Arlette smiled politely. "Such a poor, dumb brute. He's more like an oversized dog than a human being, but he does have his uses."

Fargo did not bother to comment. The more he saw of the illustrious countess, the less he liked her. She had the uppity air of someone too big for her britches. But then, blue bloods were forever looking down their noses at those who were not in their high-and-mighty social class.

"Cat got your tongue, sir?" Arlette said. "Or is your silence merely an indication that you are as laconic by habit as most of your backwoods breed?"

The thinly veiled insult sparked Fargo into replying, "I'm not one of those who flap their gums just to hear themselves talk, if that's what you mean."

"Touché," Countess Conover said, her eyes twinkling. "You Americans unsheathe your claws at the slightest provocation, don't you?"

"Ask the British," Fargo retorted.

Arlette laughed, her mirth as musical as her voice, as alluring as her provocative figure. She had to be cold in her sheer dress, but she did not act as if she were. Tossing her raven mane, she said, "Perhaps you will prove more interesting than the last frontiersman who stopped here. Such a dolt he was, and an utter bore. He even had the gall to paw me as if I were a common strumpet. But Mr. Flint learned."

"Flint? Jasper Flint?" Fargo said. The man in question was a former riverboat ruffian who lived by his wits and his brawn. They had run into one another on occasion. Two or three times they had dueled at poker. The last Fargo knew, Flint had planned to try his hand at prospecting.

"You knew him?" Countess Conover said. "My, the company you kept. The man was a pig."

Flint had been rough around the edges, but Fargo would not brand him so harshly. "He's just fond of pretty females," he remarked. A fondness they had shared. He turned on hearing hooves clatter on stone, and Jim Conover, now wearing a heavy coat and broad-brimmed brown hat, rode out leading a spare mount by the reins. "Climb on the hurricane deck, friend, and we'll rustle up your own critter in no time."

Arlette lifted a slender hand. "Be back in time for the evening meal, James. I'll have Maline set an extra plate for your guest."

"Will do, love of my life," Conover quipped, at which his wife turned on her heel and departed, her hips swaying enticingly. "Isn't she something special?" he said, winking at Fargo.

"That's one way of putting it," Fargo said dryly, swinging the sorrel to the west and applying his heels. Trotting to the rise, he bore to the north, paralleling the tree line, hoping to strike the Ovaro's trail at some point.

Jim Conover rode alongside, chatting amiably. "I can't tell you how grand it is to have someone stay over. It's too isolated out here for my tastes."

"Then why stay?" Fargo asked offhandedly, scouring the carpet of snow ahead. They were losing light fast. Soon it would be too dark to track.

"Arlette is fond of this spot. The setting reminds her of the Swiss Alps, where her first husband had a castle a lot like this one, only bigger." Conover paused. "Or was it her third husband? I keep getting them all mixed up." He paused again. "She's from France, in case you haven't guessed."

"You're not," Fargo observed.

Conover chuckled. "No, sir. Homegrown Kansan, that's me. It's hard to believe that three years ago I was a dry-goods clerk, barely earning enough to get by, and now I have more money than I know what to do with."

Fargo could not resist. "I'll bet your wife knows what to do with it."

Guffawing loudly, Jim Conover smacked his thigh in merriment. "Isn't that the truth! I swear that the Good Lord put women on this earth just to bankrupt us men! She spends it almost as fast as I earn it." Twisting, he gazed rather sadly at the stark battlements. "This whole setup was her notion. I was content living in Denver. Plenty of fine restaurants there, the best of private clubs, theaters, and the opera. What more could anyone want?"

A line of broken snow in the distance was of more interest to Fargo. He brought the sorrel to a gallop. Soon he was looking at tracks made by shod hooves, tracks he knew as well as he did his own footprints.

"Your pinto?" Jim asked.

Fargo nodded. The stallion was heading eastward at a brisk walk. It had passed that spot over half an hour ago. They would be hard pressed to overtake it, but he was determined to try.

Scattered clusters of trees fringed Castle Conover to the north. East of it thick forest resumed. They plunged into a twilight realm, moving in single file, Fargo in the lead. He reined up so sharply that the Kansan nearly collided with him.

"What's the matter, friend?"

The problem was a new set of hoofprints. Or, more precisely, *five* new sets that rushed from cover to surround the Ovaro's. The snow had been trampled flat, the ground torn by a struggle.

"Damn!" Fargo fumed, dismounting to examine the sign more closely.

Jim Conover was not much of a tracker. "Why are you so upset?" he asked. "Did something happen to your pinto?"

"Utes have him."

"Utes!" Conover exclaimed in horror. "Are you sure?"

Fargo pointed out the details. "Five warriors were heading southwest toward their village when they spotted my stallion and hid behind those pines. You can see where their unshod mounts broke those branches. They surrounded the Ovaro. It tried to break away, but one of them caught hold of the bridle while two others hemmed it in."

"Goodness gracious!" Jim exclaimed. "We were warned that it was folly to build our winter home so far from the settlements, but Arlette wouldn't listen. So far the Indians have left us pretty much alone."

"Pretty much?"

"Last fall six warriors pitched camp outside our walls. One of them spoke a little English. I went out to palaver. His people were upset that we had built our place on Ute land without their say-so. He said that if we wanted to stay, we had to pay tribute to the tribe. A cow every six months would be enough. I agreed, but I told him I had to talk it over with my wife first, and I'd let him know in the morning."

Fargo rose. The tracks roved to the southeast, as if the band had fought shy of the castle for some reason. "What did she say?"

Conover scrunched up his face as would a man who had just sucked a lemon. "That's the strange part. Arlette has a temper, and she made it plain that she was not about to give in to a bunch of thieving heathens, as she called them. I tried to explain that the Indians were in the right, but she wouldn't listen. She told me to go to bed, that the Utes would be gone in the morning." Conover snorted. "Damned if they weren't, too. One of the most peculiar things I've ever seen."

Fargo had a decision to make. The sun was gone. In no time it would be pitch black out, since there would be no moon. He might be able to track the Utes, but it would be slow going, and he risked losing their trail. Common sense dictated that he wait until morning, then push himself to his limit to ensure they did not get away.

"The Indians won't go very far today, will they?" Conover inquired nervously. "I mean, I've heard tell that they don't do much traveling or raiding at night. Something to do with the souls of their dead, I think."

The man had a point, Fargo mused. It was highly unlikely the band would travel all night. And it was equally unlikely the Utes would harm the Ovaro. A magnificent horse like the stallion was worth its weight in repeating rifles. "I guess I'll take you up on your offer of a place to stay the night," he said. "That is, if it's still good?"

The Kansan showed more teeth than a patent medicine salesman. "Are you serious? It will be marvelous to have someone else to talk to besides Arlette and the servants. But I warn you. It's been so long since we've had company that I'm liable to bend your ear until the wee hours."

"Fair enough," Fargo said. A little conversation was a small price to pay for a hot meal and a soft bed. He felt sorry for his host, stuck in the middle of the mountains with a domineering wife, a mute manservant, and a bevy of maids and the like. Which reminded him. "How many people live in Castle Conover?"

"Let's see. Me. Arlette. Quirinoc. Then there's our maid, Maline. Our cook, Beverly. Cheeves, who doesn't seem to do much all day except walk around dusting the furniture. And Cass, our stable man. That makes seven." Conover snapped his fingers. "Oh. And Albion, my wife's secretary. I hardly ever see much of him and tend to forget he's even around."

"What does your wife need a secretary for?"

The Kansan shrugged. "Beats the hell out of me. I asked my wife once, and she told me to mind my own business.

Near as I can gather, he answers her correspondence and conducts certain business transactions on her behalf." Conover reined his animal to the west. "Come on. Let's suffer through supper, then retire to my study. I'll treat you to whiskey that will go down as smooth as silk."

Resigned to giving up for the moment, Fargo goaded the sorrel into step next to the bay. He looked back several times, praying that he was not making a mistake he would regret the rest of his life.

Jim Conover rubbed his hands with glee. "This is my fondest wish come true! I can't stand—" Suddenly gasping, he exclaimed, "My word!"

Fargo heard it as well. A strident wail of terror that rent the dark from the vicinity of Castle Conover.

32

3

"Good God!" Jim Conover cried. "That must be Arlette!" Slapping his legs against the bay, he galloped toward the sound.

Skye Fargo jabbed his spurs into the sorrel and shot past the wealthy eccentric. The wail rose to a high-pitched shriek. Sweeping around a stand of pines, he saw a pair of struggling figures.

At first glance the short hairs at the nape of Fargo's neck prickled. One of the figures was a young woman in a white dress. But the other was a towering scarecrow of a man with white skin and a shock of unruly white hair. The scarecrow had his hands around the pretty woman's throat and was savagely shaking her.

Fargo did not call out to them. He did not stop and demand to know what was going on. Like a bolt out of the blue he swept down on the pair, slipping his right boot from its stirrup. At the last instant the scarecrow must have heard the drum of hooves, and he started to run.

Fargo's boot slammed into the man's chest with the force of a battering ram. The figure catapulted backward into the snow, rolled a few times, then heaved off the ground. Before the scarecrow could lift an arm, Fargo launched himself from the saddle and tore into the woman's assailant with flying fists. His right smashed into the lean goblin's jaw; his left drove to the elbow into the man's stomach.

The scarecrow went down a second time. Fargo cocked

his fists, braced to ward off an attack, but the white figure made no attempt to come to grips with him. Instead, the man rose onto his elbows, his pink eyes glaring balefully.

Pink? With a start, Fargo realized the man was an albino. The man's lean six-and-a-half-foot frame was clothed in ordinary although expensive clothes and short black leather boots. Fargo glanced at the albino's hands, figuring to find long, tapered fingernails, but they were shorter than his own. So this could not possibly be the madman who had attacked him during the storm. "On your feet," he growled.

Just then the bay arrived in a flurry of spraying snow. Jim Conover looked from the trembling woman to the albino. "Albion! What is the meaning of this? Why were you manhandling Beverly?"

Fargo slowly stepped back. Albion was the name of the countesses's male secretary. Beverly was the cook. He wondered if maybe the pair had been having a lovers' quarrel.

The woman responded before the albino could, saying fearfully, "It was nothing, Mr. Conover! Just a little misunderstanding."

"But he was strangling you!" Conover said. "I saw it with my own eyes."

Beverly was ashen. She nervously licked her full red lips, then gave her burnished sandy tresses a shake and said, "No, no. You have it all wrong, sir. He was shaking me, is all. I'm fine. No harm was done."

It did not take a genius to tell she was lying. Fargo saw it right away, but apparently his host was much more gullible.

"Even so, his conduct will not be tolerated," Conover said, and wagged a finger at the albino, who was rising and brushing himself off. "Albion, you will report to my study after supper and give an account of your actions. I don't care if you are my wife's pet. I hired Beverly myself, and I'll be damned if I'll let you or anyone else abuse her!"

Albion finally spoke, his voice resonant and cultured. "My profound apologies, your lordship—"

"I'm not a lord and you know it!" Conover cut him off. "My wife might be partial to her fancy titles, but you will address me as I've told you to."

Fargo was a keen judge of human character. He had to be, in order to survive. And what he saw reflected in the hellish depths of the albino's smoldering pink eyes did not bode well for the master of the castle. Yet Albion did not betray the volcanic violence that boiled under the surface of his cultured veneer.

"As you wish, Mr. Conover, sir. Again, my apologies. I meant no disrespect." Uncoiling to his full height, he shifted his gaze to Fargo. "And you must be the gentleman my mistress mentioned. The cowboy."

The last word was uttered with thinly veiled contempt. "I don't herd cattle for a living," Fargo said, setting him straight.

"Oh? Then what do you do, if I might be permitted to ask?"

Fargo did many things, and did them well. One week he might be scouting for the army, the next searching for someone lost in the wilderness, the next helping to guide a lost wagon train. And there was something else he did, better than anyone, anywhere. "Sometimes I hunt down bastards like you when they step outside the law."

Beverly gasped. Jim Conover recoiled. But the albino, oddly enough, did not bat an eye. Calmly adjusting his sleeves, Albion replied, "How interesting, sir. I'll be sure to keep it in mind. Now if you'll excuse me?"

The last was addressed to Conover, who absently nodded. The secretary walked off with an exaggerated swagger, like a great prowling cat. When Albion was out of earshot, Conover muttered, "I never have liked that man."

Beverly was fussing with her hair, unconscious of how her white uniform clung suggestively to her ample form. The swell of her bosom was twice that of most women. Her pearly legs were exposed to above the knee, and Fargo speculated on whether her thighs were as fine as the rest of her.

Conover seemed oblivious to her charms. "Beverly, what in the name of all that's holy were you doing out here by yourself? Don't you know it's dangerous, what with Indians and bears and the like?"

She pointed at several short dead limbs near her feet. "I needed wood for the stove. Normally, I don't stray this far from the castle. But with the snow covering everything . . ." She left the statement unfinished.

"If you want, I'll insist that my wife fire Albion," Conover offered. "He had no business treating you as he did."

Raw fear etched Beverly's features, fear she quickly tried to hide. "No, please! Don't go to any bother on my account! It won't happen again. Let's just drop it."

"I don't know if I should," Conover said uncertainly.

"Please, sir!" Beverly insisted, in her extremity placing a hand on the lord of the manor's leg.

Jim Conover gave in. Patting her head as a father might his daughter, he said, "Very well. It's against my better judgment. But if he ever again so much as lays a finger on you, you are to tell me right away. Understood?"

Beverly nodded. "Thank you," she said gratefully, then squatted to collect the wood. The hem of her uniform slid up, revealing silken thighs every bit as tantalizing as Fargo had suspected. "Now I'd better hurry. Your wife will have a fit if I don't finish the meal on time."

"Allow me," Fargo said, bending to pick up the branches first. They both reached for the same limb and their fingers accidentally brushed together. It sent a warm tingle up his arm. "I'll walk you back to make sure you get there safely."

"There's no need," Beverly said.

"Yes, there is," Fargo said and nodded to the east. "We found Ute sign over yonder."

The mere mention of the scourge of the Rockies brought Beverly to her feet, her back stiff, a hand to her throat. "Utes! I knew they wouldn't leave us alone!"

Fargo rose with the wood in his arms. "Jim, why don't you take the sorrel on back. We'll be there soon."

"All right," Conover said. "But if you run into any trouble, fire a shot and I'll come running with Quirinoc. The Indians are scared to death of him." Snatching the sorrel's reins, he trotted off and was soon lost in the darkness.

The sudden silence was unnerving. Except for the groaning wind, the Rockies were as deathly still as a cemetery at midnight. To the north and west jagged peaks thrust darkly upward as if trying to impale the stars.

Fargo gathered more wood as they walked. He noticed Beverly studying him when she thought he would not see.

They had gone a short way when she cleared her throat. "I want to thank you for what you did. Not many men would have the courage to take on Albion. You've made a bitter enemy there."

"I've made enemies before," Fargo mentioned. He did not bother to point out that most of them wound up buzzard bait.

That was the way of things on the frontier. Unlike back East, where everyone settled their disputes in court, in the West a man was expected to stand up for himself. Relying on lawyers was the last resort of those made weak-kneed by all the laws passed by lawyer politicians to force people into fattening their wallets.

"I'm Beverly Shannon, by the way," she said. "I know who you are. Maline, the maid, told me. She and the others can't stop talking about you. It isn't often that we have a visitor."

"How long ago did Jasper Flint stop by?"

Abruptly stopping, Beverly said breathlessly, "Are you a friend of his?"

"Not hardly. The countess mentioned that he had been here." Fargo was puzzled by the expression of unbridled terror that had come over her. She covered it by adopting a wan smile.

"That's nice to know. Mr. Flint had hung around too

many saloons. He seemed to think that women are only interested in one thing."

"Men are," Fargo quipped, grinning and winking.

Shannon laughed lustily, her glorious mounds bouncing up and down. "Don't I know it. You're honest, Mr. Fargo, as well as brave. Strange that a handsome man with your character doesn't have himself a wife."

Fargo had to admire her tactful prying. "Call me Skye," he said. "I'm not in the market for a wife, and don't think I'll ever be." Another log was added to his growing collection as he did some prying of his own. "How long have you worked for Conover?"

"A couple of years now," Beverly revealed. "I knew him before he made his big silver strike, back in Idaho Springs, where I ran a restaurant. He ate there every day. We got acquainted fairly well. Strictly as friends, you understand."

Fargo believed her. From what he had seen of Conover, the man did not have much experience with the fairer sex.

"Then Jim struck it big," Beverly went on, "and I didn't see much of him for the longest time. He was too busy setting up his mine and whatnot." A tinge of resentment crept into her tone. "The next thing I heard, he had gone to Europe to take in the sights and somehow or other wound up with a spanking new bride—the countess."

There was no love lost between Shannon and Arlette, if Fargo was any judge. Was it a case of simple jealousy, or something deeper?

"You could have floored me with a feather when Jim popped in one day and asked me to come work for him as his personal cook," Beverly disclosed. "I declined at first. I was happy running my own eatery. My folks ran one in Ohio before we moved west."

"But he wouldn't take no for an answer?" Fargo prompted when she grew wistfully quiet.

Beverly idly clasped her arms to her chest, which had the unintended effect of swelling her breasts like overripe melons. "He kept pestering me, offering me more and more money, until it got to the point where I would have been a fool to refuse. He was so happy, he had tears in his eyes."

"Do you like working for him?"

"For Jim, yes." Beverly paused as if debating whether to say more. She did. "He'd told me that his wife insisted he hire a full staff of servants. That if he didn't, she would pack up and go back to Europe. I should have taken that as a warning of things to come."

They were nearing Castle Conover. Beverly, about to elaborate, tilted her head and gave a start.

Fargo glanced at the ramparts, where perched on a parapet was the dark silhouette of a female figure, her hair blowing wildly in the wind. Was she spying on them? Whether it was Arlette or another he could not say. The woman stepped back from view the instant that he saw her.

Beverly was clearly upset. "I don't know how much more of this I can take. As fond as I am of Jim, I'd rather go back to working for myself."

So saying, Shannon hurried on around the northwest corner to the recessed iron door. A large key attached to her belt opened it. She pressed both hands against the heavy portal and strained.

Fargo added his muscles to the effort. The hinges needed oiling badly. Before them unfolded a long, narrow, murky corridor lit at intervals by lanterns nestled in sheltered nooks. A dank, musty scent permeated the air.

After locking the door, Beverly beckoned and led Fargo to the third room on the right. It turned out to be a spacious kitchen, well illuminated, the walls laden with pots and pans and sundry other utensils. The fragrant aroma of brewing coffee made Fargo's mouth water. Vegetables boiled on the stove. Roasting in the oven were several plump grouse.

"Over there," Beverly said, pointing at a small stack of wood in the corner.

Fargo added his armful. As he uncoiled, he spotted a familiar picnic basket on a table against the far wall.

Following his gaze, Beverly blurted, "How in the world

did that get there? It wasn't when I left. Someone must have brought it in while I was gone." Walking over, she raised the lid and shook her head in surprise. "Look at all this food. Someone raided the pantry without telling me. But who would want to go on a picnic with all that snow outside?"

Fargo kept his little secret to himself. Striding toward the corridor, he said, "I'm going to find Jim." As he faced front, into the kitchen whirled a human tornado. A lithe blonde in a skimpy black uniform nearly bowled him over. Her breasts mashed against his chest, her arms going around his waist as she grabbed him to keep from losing her balance. A scent of lavender clung to her shiny thick locks.

"*Pardon, monsieur!*" the newcomer exclaimed in a thick accent. "Please forgive me! I did not see you."

"No harm done," Fargo said, boldly raking her from head to toe with a knowing appraisal. She was not as amply endowed as Beverly Shannon, nor an exotic beauty like Arlette Conover, but she was spectacular in her own right. Her every movement, her every pose, was unintentionally provocative. Fargo's mouth watered again, for an entirely different reason. "I haven't had the pleasure," he remarked.

"Maline Bonacieux," she said, blushing at the hunger he did not try to hide. "I know who you are, of course. My mistress says that I am to see that you have whatever you need." She curtsied primly, but her eyes lit with mischief. "I am the maid, *monsieur.*"

"And a prettier maid I've never met," Fargo bluntly responded. Her blush deepened, and her eyelids fluttered, provoking a stirring in his loins.

"*Merci,*" Maline said. "You are the *gallant*, no? The last man who stayed here did not have your manners. He was a great brute."

"So I keep hearing," Fargo said. It occurred to him that she still had her arms around his waist. He ran a finger along one from her wrist to her elbow, eliciting a tiny shudder of raw desire. "I hope we get to see each other again."

"Whatever the *monsieur* wants," Maline said impishly.

Beverly Shannon was tapping a toe in impatience. "Maline, if you can manage to pry yourself off him, I need help getting this meal done on time."

"*Oui, mon ami*," the maid said, sidestepping sweetly and bowing again. "Later, *monsieur*."

Smiling to himself, Fargo ambled out. He turned right and soon came to where the corridor forked. Only then did it dawn on him that he had neglected to ask for directions.

Straight ahead another sixty feet the corridor ended at a large closed door. Advancing, Fargo tried the latch, but it was either locked or bolted on the other side. He rapped loudly and no one answered. About to retrace his steps, he paused when a scraping sound issued from the other side. A peculiar sense of dread came over him, a blind conviction that whatever made that noise was unspeakably sinister.

His Colt seemed to jump into his hand of its own accord. The latch moved, and his skin crawled. Someone was trying to open the door. With bated breath he waited, thumb on the hammer. He could not say why, but relief washed over him when the latch became still.

In the tense quiet Fargo could hear the hammering of his own heart. He also heard a shuffling tread, faint but distinct. Whatever had worked the latch was leaving.

Fargo backed up to the fork. Twirling the pistol into his holster, he angled to the right. In twenty yards a wide flight of dimly lit stone stairs spiraled up into even dimmer heights. His nerves on edge, he climbed.

No one had ever mentioned to him how dank and chill castles were. For the life of him, Fargo could not imagine why anyone would want to live in one. He preferred the wide open spaces. Give him sunlight and fresh air any day over the dreary confines of the sprawling stone monstrosity the Conovers called home.

He could not help but wonder if Jim Conover liked it any better. Building the monumental waste of time and money had been Arlette's idea, after all. Fargo guessed that she was trying to re-create the life she had enjoyed in the old country, at her newest husband's expense.

The stairs brought him to a broad hall of gigantic proportions that ran the length of the castle. Dense shadows cloaked the walls and the ceiling. Plush rugs had been thrown down at random. Around them and on them clustered mahogany and oaken furniture. The gleam of candles flickered in candelabra, which cast writhing shapes on the floor.

Fargo had taken only a few steps into the open when he halted, his wilderness-honed instincts sensing that he was not alone. He scanned the hall, then turned to the flight of masterfully crafted stairs that led to the next floor.

A hint of movement at the top galvanized Fargo into springing upward. His long legs took the three steps at a stride. He gained the landing in seconds. Yet when he got there, the upper corridor was empty. All the doors were closed. No sounds wafted from any of them.

Fargo decided he was getting too jumpy for his own good. He moved to the edge of the landing, surprised there was no rail, and gazed out over the immense hall. Near the far end, lost in a vista of choking shadow, a pale shape flitted to a doorway and disappeared.

The albino, Fargo reasoned, and turned to go down. But someone stood almost at his elbow, blocking his way. He recoiled, nearly resorting to his Colt until he recognized the hulking, silent figure whose lone eye danced with inner fire.

Fargo was impressed. Rarely was anyone able to sneak up on him unnoticed. Granted, soft soles would not make much noise on the smooth stone floor, but he should have heard *something*, or at least registered the faint stirring of air that marked the passage of a large body. Yet he'd had no inkling of the hunchback's presence.

"Quirinoc," Fargo said, nodding. "What can I do for you?"

42

The manservant indicated the stairs and started down, his awkward gait made more so.

Fargo was astounded. Those thick stunted legs moved as noiselessly as an Apache's. At the bottom Quirinoc slanted across the hall to a corridor Fargo had not realized was there. A Turkish tapestry was to blame. The hunchback held it open so Fargo could go through, then trailed him to a door from which rosy light poured.

It was the dining room. A table seemingly the length of a city block had been polished to a fine sheen. Jim Conover sat at one end, glumly sipping scotch. He was the only one there, although plates and silverware had been set for two others. As Fargo entered, Conover brightened.

"There you are! I hope you don't mind my sending Quirinoc to find you. I was afraid you might get lost. This damn place is a maze."

Fargo made a beeline for a selection of full liquor bottles and empty crystal glasses on a silver tray. He helped himself to three fingers of whiskey, downed it in a single gulp, then poured another.

"So what do you think of Conover's Folly, as the locals in Georgetown call it?" his host inquired.

"Just between you and me," Fargo said, "I wouldn't live here for all the precious ore in the Rockies."

Conover sighed. "You loathe it, too? Sometimes I think that the only one who likes this clammy dump is my wife. What she sees in it, I'll never know."

Taking a seat on the silver magnate's right, Fargo gestured at the vacant expanse of tabletop. "Why only three plates? Don't the servants get to eat with us?"

"I wish." Conover morosely swirled his scotch. "I know that I'd enjoy their company. But Arlette would brand it preposterous for the hired help to eat with their betters. She never stops reminding me that we have to keep them in their place."

Just as she did with the Utes, Fargo reflected bitterly. It was too bad the woman had not been born an Indian.

Maybe then she would have more respect for others. He changed the subject. "I've been meaning to ask. What can you tell me about the wild man who attacked me during the snowstorm?"

Conover's eyebrows met over his nose. "What the dickens are you talking about? There are no wild men in these parts that I know of."

As if to prove Conover wrong, from the depths of the castle wavered a bestial wolfish howl.

4

The howl rose to a feverish pitch. It seemed to echo and re-echo off the walls, growing louder and louder until Fargo would have sworn that whatever made it was right outside the dining room. He flung himself from his chair and was out the doorway in a rush.

Coming down the gloomy corridor was a shadowy shape. Fargo's right hand stabbed for his Colt, but he checked his draw when the figure passed under a lantern.

Countess Arlette Leonie Mignon d'Arcy Conover wore a taunting smile, and little else. Her dress was so sheer, so thin, that it clung to her like a second skin. The fabric was new to Fargo. It shimmered with a thousand tiny pinpoints of light as the lantern glow bathed it. And he could see *through* it when the light was just right. The swell of her full breasts with their button nipples, the inward curve of her flat belly, the dark thatch at the junction of her velvet thighs, all were as plain as day.

The lord of the castle came puffing out of the dining room just as the howl ended. "Arlette! My love!" he blurted. "Did you hear that awful sound?"

"What of it, husband dearest?" the countess replied, not at all concerned. "There must be wolves outside again."

Fargo's skepticism must have shown, because she looked at him and her grin widened. "Believe it or not, Mr. Fargo, there are wolves in these mountains. From time to time they come out of the deep woods, gather on the rise west of here, and howl their hairy hearts out for hours on end. It scares our poor cook and our maid to death, but I find their lupine chorus quite pleasing to the ear."

Jim Conover swore half under his breath. "You might. I sure don't. If they're so close that they can make us jump out of our skins, maybe I should have Cass go up on the ramparts and pick a few off with his rifle."

"Nonsense, James," Arlette said as she brushed past him, her long fingernail tracing the outline of his plump chin. "The wolves aren't hurting anyone. Leave them be." She entered the room with him glued to her heels, like an overfed dog tagging behind its stern master.

Fargo was not fooled for an instant. He could not begin to count the number of wolves he had heard in full throat over the years. He knew every note they were capable of, knew the range of their vocal ability better than anyone. Which was why he was sure that whatever uttered that howl had not been a wolf. It had sounded almost . . . human.

A commotion in the room drew Fargo in. Through a door on the west side Maline had appeared, pushing a cart laden with trays of steaming food. She gave him a quick, teasing glance, then began placing the trays on the long table.

Arlette had taken her seat on her husband's left. Jim was pouring his third scotch, and this time he did not add any water. As he sipped, his wife frowned and tapped a finger in annoyance.

"Be careful, James. At the rate you're going, you're liable to turn into a drunk before spring. Must you drink so much, especially when we have company?"

Fargo's sympathy for the miserable man was growing by the hour. In all his travels he'd never met a more henpecked spouse. To take some of the heat off the Kansan, he strolled to the liquor tray, opened a whiskey bottle, and raised it in salute, saying, "Don't stop drinking on my account, Jim. Hell, every man should have a few now and then." To demonstrate his point, he drank direct from the bottle, gulping healthy mouthfuls, then smacking his lips with relish.

The countess was not amused. "Honestly, Mr. Fargo, I expected you to have better manners than our last guest, Jasper Flint."

At the mention of the former riverman's name, Maline, who was setting a bowl of cooked carrots down, bumped a glass and sent it crashing to the floor. It shattered into shards, and she paled as if she had committed a cardinal sin.

Arlette glared. "Clumsiness will not be tolerated, Miss Bonacieux. You know that. The cost of the glass will be deducted from your pay."

"Whatever you say, *madam*," Maline said contritely. "I am sorry. We are running a little behind, and I am hurrying to set up."

"That's right," the countess said, consulting a grandfather clock in the corner. "Supper is five minutes late. Inform Miss Shannon that I will also dock her pay an appropriate amount."

"*Oui, madam.*"

Jim Conover slapped his glass onto the table so hard that scotch sloshed over the top. "Like hell you will, Arlette. It's not Beverly's fault the meal isn't on time. If your damned albino had not manhandled her when she was out gathering wood, she would have had supper done sooner."

Arlette went as rigid as a board. "What's that about Albion?"

"You heard me," Jim declared. "Fargo and I caught him abusing her. There is no excuse for what he did. I won't abide it."

Confusion replaced Arlette's smug demeanor.

"If you want Albion to stay on, I suggest you set him straight on how folks behave in this country," Jim said. "I aim to have a few words with him myself." His wife flushed and would have objected, but he cut her off. "I know! I know! I've heard it all before. How he's been your personal secretary for over ten years. How you simply can't get by without him." Jim's voice lifted in rare anger. "But this is *my* home and he's paid with *my* money, so he can damn well act decently or I'll have him shipped back to Europe so fast, his head will spin. Is that clear?"

It was the first time Fargo had witnessed Conover stand up to his wife. Judging by her amazement and the maid's stunned look, it was the first time they had seen it, too.

"*Is that clear?*" Jim practically yelled when the countess did not reply.

Given Arlette's temperament, Fargo expected her to tear into the Kansan like an enraged she-cat. To his surprise, though, she turned scarlet, grit her teeth, then appeared to wrestle inwardly with her temper. After a bit she bowed her head and said in a soft tone, "Whatever you think is best, husband. The last thing I ever want to do is upset you."

Fargo would have waged good money that she was not sincere, but Jim Conover melted like putty. Moving around to her chair, he gave her a tender hug while pecking her cheek.

"Now look at what I've done! I'm sorry, my dear. I shouldn't take out my frustrations on you."

Arlette looked up. Fargo, sitting across from her, wondered why it was that her husband did not notice the wicked gleam of triumph in her eyes.

"Think no more of it, James. Albion will behave himself, I assure you. And I will insist that he give Miss Shannon a formal apology."

By then the meal had been served. The Conovers turned to their food, making small talk that held little interest for Fargo. He was busy attacking dishes with gusto: seasoned grouse, potatoes, vegetables, freshly made bread, delicious butter and cakes and sweetmeats. It was food literally fit for a king, a rare treat he made the most of. Five helpings later his stomach was fit to burst.

Stiff black coffee washed everything down. Fargo was on his third cup before his hosts were done eating. Jim had eaten heartily, but his wife picked at her food as if she were troubled.

While Maline cleared the table, Arlette fixed Fargo with a stare that would have done justice to a python. "My husband has informed me of the theft of your horse. I understand that you will be leaving in the morning to go after the Utes by yourself?"

Fargo grunted, having just stuffed a last handful of sweetmeats into his mouth.

"I take that as yes. But is it wise? Jim says there are five of them. It would be the height of folly to go after them alone. Take Quirinoc along to help you. He's dealt with savages before."

When? Fargo wanted to ask, but he was still chewing away. To his knowledge, the only time the hunchback had ever seen Indians had been when the Utes paid the castle a visit months ago. He gulped the sweetmeats down, swilled the last of his coffee to clear his throat, and replied, "I don't need any help, thanks. If I do it right, I can get my horse back without bloodshed."

"Why bother?" Arlette said. "They're heathens, aren't they? It will be no great loss to the world if you were to kill all five. Do so, with my blessing."

Fargo was growing mighty tired of her pompous airs. "I don't need your blessing to do anything," he reminded her. "And those heathens you hate so much are a lot like you and me. The color of their skin is different, and they don't live like we do, but they are human beings just the same."

The countess found it humorous. "Really, Mr. Fargo? How quaint. I suppose you would say the same of primitive blacks who dwell in squalid huts in deepest Africa? Or of those slant-eyed yellow devils over in China?"

Anger boiled up in Fargo. Bigots always brought a bitter taste to his mouth. Little did Arlette Conover know that he had lived among a number of Indian tribes. That he had shared their lodges and their food. That he had fought with them and loved their women. And he'd stack any one of them up against the bitch across the table. "People are people," he stressed.

"More homespun philosophy?" Arlette subtly mocked him. "Well, I happen to know better. Some people are naturally superior to others."

"How so?" Fargo challenged her.

"In every way imaginable," Arlette sniffed. "Take me, for example. I was educated in the best schools money could buy. I was bred to culture. I speak five languages. I can sculpt and paint and recite poetry by the hour. Can a pathetic red squaw do any of that?"

"No," Fargo conceded. "But most are experts at sewing and beadwork and tanning hides. They keep their families fed and clothed as best they can, which isn't always easy. And I've met plenty who can speak tongues other than their own."

Gay laughter fluttered from the countess. "Why, there is no comparison! You have made my case for me."

Fargo never struck women unless in self-defense, but he sorely wished he could haul off and punch Arlette Conover smack on her jaw. She deserved it. The woman grated on him like sand on metal.

Jim turned to the Trailsman and slid a thick cigar from an inner pocket. "How about if we retire to my study? I'd love to hear the latest news from the outside world."

The countess put her hand on her husband's arm. "Hold on a moment. Don't you remember giving me your word that you would sign those business papers before we turned in tonight? Albion left them on your desk." She smiled politely at Fargo. "I'm sure our guest would rather rest after his tiring day. Maline can show him to his room."

"*Oui!*" the maid bubbled. "I would be very happy to."

Conover squirmed. "Damn it all. Can't those infernal papers wait one more day?"

"No, they can't," Arlette insisted. "You're the head of a vast financial empire now, not a common clerk. You have responsibilities you cannot shirk." She snapped her fingers at the maid. "What are you waiting for? Escort Mr. Fargo upstairs. You know which room."

Maline Bonacieux curtsied, then bestowed a hungry grin on Fargo as he rose and followed her out. No sooner were they through the doorway than the Conovers started arguing. Jim accused Arlette of treating him as if he were a child, and she retorted that if it were not for her, his empire would have collapsed long ago.

The maid sighed. "They fight like this all the time, *monsieur*," she confided. "Like . . . how you say . . . *ze* cats and *ze* dogs?"

"That's how we say it, all right." Fargo was aroused by the saucy swing to her hips as she pranced before him. Her rich blond hair bounced with every graceful step, and when she twisted to smile at him, he could not help but appreciate how her firm breasts pushed against her skimpy black uniform.

"My English is not as good as it should be sometimes," Maline said. "The countess forever scolds me for not trying hard enough."

"She should talk," Fargo said. They were nearing the great hall, when without any hint that he was there, Quirinoc stepped from an inky nook, barring their way.

Maline recoiled, sliding next to Fargo and gripping his arm so tight her nails dug into his skin. "What do you want?" she demanded timidly. "I am on an errand for your mistress."

The hunchback's single eye gleamed as he regarded her closely, then stared at Fargo. His rippling muscles twitched, his ham-sized fists knotted. Invisible energy seemed to crackle in the corridor, as if the massive manservant were about to explode with violence.

"Go away!" Maline said. "Or I will tell the countess on you!"

Quirinoc's jaws flexed; the folds of flesh quivered. But he slunk obediently off into the great hall, the colorful tapestry closing behind him.

Fargo felt the maid tremble. "What was that all about? Has he been giving you trouble?"

"No," Maline said, much too readily. "But I catch him staring at me often from the shadows. When I complain to the *madam*, she says to ignore him, that he is an overgrown puppy."

More like an unpredictable grizzly, Fargo thought, but he kept the observation to himself. Since she acted skittish about going on, he took her hand and the lead. Throwing the tapestry aside, he stepped into the hall.

The hunchback had vanished. Fargo peered into every shadow, scrutinized every doorway. There had not been time for Quirinoc to cross to the stairs or reach any of the other corridors, but he was nowhere to be found. "Where did he get to?"

Maline tossed her golden hair. "I have no idea. He does that a lot. So does Albion. Sometimes I feel their eyes on me as I go about my chores. But when I look, *zey* are not there." She gazed anxiously at the looming darkness that clung to the high ceiling. "To tell the truth, *monsieur*, I do not like this place."

"Then why stay?"

"Why else? The money. The countess pays extremely well. In one month I earn what would take six months back in France. I save most of it, and in two years I will have enough to buy a nice home on the Seine."

Fargo mulled her response as they crossed to the wide stone steps. Beverly Shannon stayed on for the same reason. No one could accuse the Conovers of being stingy with their wealth.

Maline's spiked heels clicked on the stone as they climbed. She had regained her brash confidence and several times her shoulder brushed his arm suggestively. Her perfume, a sharp musky scent, helped fuel the craving she stirred.

At the first landing she walked to the left, passing several rooms. As they went by an open door, Fargo happened to glance inside.

Shelves crammed with books lined every wall from floor

to ceiling. A plush burgundy carpet complemented drapes of the same color. A large mahogany desk sat in the center, two easy chairs in front of it. Behind the desk, bent over a foot-high stack of papers, was the albino. Albion held a single sheet in his left hand, one corner bearing a red mark of some kind. He was intently sorting through the pile.

Fargo slowed, curious. The scarecrow inserted the single sheet, then hastily straightened the stack. Glancing up, Albion spotted them. A smirk spread over his pasty features.

Maline had not paid any attention to the secretary. At the second door past the study she halted and coyly pivoted, her bosom a hair's width from his chest, her lively blue eyes framing a question that had nothing to do with the one she voiced aloud. "Well, here is your room, *monsieur*. Will that be all?"

"I could use a nightcap," Fargo said. "Any chance of having a bottle brought up?"

The maid was thrilled. "*Oui*. I will bring it myself. Say, in fifteen minutes?" She skipped off, whistling to herself.

Fargo shoved on the heavy oak door. The same burgundy carpet covered the floor. A four-poster bed dominated the center. To the right was a polished dresser, to the left a fireplace, the crackling logs licked by flaming fingers. A lone lantern on a small shelf provided extra light. He walked to the small window beyond the bed and parted the drapes.

A white mantle stretched for as far as the eye could see. The snow was dully radiant in the glow of pale starlight. Lighter patches were broken by somber shadows.

Fargo tensed when one of those shadows moved. Something glided swiftly along the tree line, something that flowed on two legs, upright like a man. Yet its jerky motion and the constant bobbing of its head suggested that it must be an animal. He saw it cross a pale patch, pause, and glance toward Castle Conover. Only for a heartbeat did it freeze there, then it was gone like a spooked antelope, bounding into the woods.

In that brief instant Fargo learned that it was indeed a

man. An Indian warrior, if the man's buckskins and shoulder-length dark hair were any indication. Fargo leaped to the conclusion that it must be one of the Utes. But if so, what was the warrior doing skulking around the castle so late at night? Could it be that one of them was to blame for the attack during the blizzard?

So many questions, so few answers. Fargo watched to see if the figure would reappear, but it did not. He moved to the bed to await the maid, then heard loud voices down the hall.

Maline had left the door open a crack. Fargo put his ear to it and overheard the countess saying, "—don't care how put out you are. Business is business. And you did tell the president of First National that I was free to do with the money whatever I saw fit."

"But so large a sum!" Jim Conover said. "The least you could have done is let me know ahead of time." His voice dropped and the next statement was too low to carry far. His wife answered. Resentment made him cry out, "Damn it all, Arlette! It's *my* fortune, not yours! I don't like how you treat it as your personal treasure trove, even if we are man and wife."

"Calm down, James. Someone might hear us."

"So what?" Jim snapped. "It's high time we settled this once and for all."

"I totally agree," Arlette said icily. "Come into your study and we will discuss this like civilized adults."

A door slammed. Silence reigned. Fargo stepped out into the dim corridor. From within the study rose a muffled heated exchange. He was about to move nearer when he felt another presence behind him. Not as close as the hunchback had been earlier, but close enough. He was being watched.

Fargo did not let on that he knew. Cocking his head as if he were trying to listen to the Conovers, he took another slow step forward. Casually, his right hand rose to his hip. The moment his fingers were as high as his Colt, he snaked out the pistol and spun. He wanted to catch the culprit off-guard. It worked.

Twenty feet away the hall angled to the right. Stygian shadow cloaked the spot, but not quite enough to completely conceal the tall white figure who was peering around the corner at Fargo. Pink eyes sparked as the albino hissed and whirled.

Fargo gave chase. He was sick and tired of being spied on, sick and tired of the countess and her staff treating him as if he were dirt. Albion needed to be taught a lesson in frontier manners, and Fargo was just the man to teach it.

Springing wide of the corner in case the albino intended to jump him, Fargo pivoted, swinging the Colt from side to side. An oath escaped him, and he took several more steps in bewilderment. "This can't be!" he declared.

But it was. The corridor only ran another fifteen feet. No doors opened off it. There were no openings in the stone walls or the ceiling and floor. Yet Albion was gone. The secretary had disappeared into thin air.

A nagging suspicion Fargo harbored grew stronger. After his experience with the hunchback, and in light of what Maline had told him, he suspected that Castle Conover must be honeycombed with secret passages. He'd heard that they were common in castles over in Europe, where in the old days the nobility sometimes had to hide from marauding enemies.

Carefully, Fargo approached the rear wall and ran his left hand over the smooth stones. Any hidden door was too well concealed for him to find. Irritated, he stalked back to his room, vowing to bolt the door and keep the fire going all night.

A shadow flitted across his doorway. Someone was in there.

Fargo cat-stepped to the jamb, gauged where the person must be, and hurled himself at the intruder, ready to brain whomever he found. His right hand clamped onto a slim wrist. Twinkling blue eyes met his.

"Oh! What is this? You are hurting me, *monsieur*."

"Sorry, ma'am," Fargo blurted, releasing the maid as if he'd grabbed a hot coal. "I thought you were someone else."

"No harm done, eh?" Maline Bonacieux said and rubbed her lush form against him. "I like it rough. I like it gentle." Her cherry lips pouted hungrily. "Which will it be, *grand homme*?"

5

Lust blazed in Skye Fargo, lust hotter than the crackling flames in the fireplace. The nubile maid had been stoking his passion all evening with her sly, inviting glances and the brazen brush of her ripe body against his, time and time again. He wanted her so much, it hurt. Her question was all it took to release his pent-up lust.

Looping an arm around Maline's slim waist, Fargo pulled her to him, mashing her against him so that her breasts ground into his broad chest, her thighs into his legs. She uttered a hungry moan stifled by the swoop of his mouth. Her soft lips parted. Her silken tongue darted to meet his halfway.

Maline Bonacieux was one of those rare women who were as aggressive as men when they made love. Maybe it had to do with her being French, since in Europe most people were brought up to have an open, forthright outlook on sex. The notion that lovemaking was a vile sin only to be done in the dead of night behind locked doors had not tainted her thinking.

Or maybe it was simply that Maline Bonacieux *liked* sex. Some women, strangely enough, did not. They could go through their whole lives without so much as kissing someone, and be perfectly content.

Their kind always mystified Fargo. Next to *being* alive, in his opinion making love to a woman was the single best experience life had to offer. Small wonder he drank at the trough of carnal desire every chance he got.

Now, covering Maline's right breast, he squeezed and kneaded it until the nipple became a hard nail under his palm and she was wriggling in hot abandon.

With a sweep of an arm, Fargo lifted her off the floor and carried her to the bed. Not once did he break their kiss. As he gently set her down, his hand slid between her legs and stroked them from ankle to midthigh. It set her to cooing and digging her painted fingernails into his shoulders.

Her black uniform was as soft as satin but not satan. Fargo ran his other hand all over it, rubbing her from top to bottom, side to side, setting her to panting like a bellows being stoked. "Oh, *monsieur*!" Maline gasped when he kissed her neck, then lathered her velvety skin from her jaw to the gap between her heaving mounds.

It did not take long to shuck the uniform. A half dozen buttons and the deed was done. Her lacy underthings were designed to stir male hunger, and they did just that. Fargo drank in the sight of her quivering figure, his lips gluing to hers again as he stretched out beside her.

Maline removed his hat and tossed it aside. She plucked at his gun belt until she got that off, then she hitched up his shirt so she could slip her dainty fingers underneath and rub them over his superbly muscled abdomen and powerful chest.

Meanwhile, Fargo bared her naked. Her skin shone with vitality. Her breasts arched to twin peaks. A flat stomach ended at a bushy golden thatch that topped a pair of willowy thighs. She was so exquisite, it brought a lump to his throat.

Fargo's manhood swelled until it was fit to burst. He nearly exploded when she unexpectedly lowered a hand to his groin and stroked the length of his shaft. It sent molten lava coursing through him. Greedily, he covered a nipple with his mouth and swirled it with his tongue, while kneading both globes until they swelled like rising dough.

On purpose, Fargo did not touch the core of her womanhood. Not yet, anyway. He wanted to arouse her to a fever pitch first. Lingering at her breasts, he kept his hands busy caressing her thighs, going just a little bit higher each time. She began to lift her luscious bottom off the bed, thrusting against him in measured tempo. Her nails seared his back, strayed to his hips, and lodged there. Groaning, she yanked him against her, as if seeking to spur him into consummating their union. Inwardly, Fargo grinned. Soon she would be ready.

Maline cried out when he nibbled a path from her breasts to her navel, then from her navel to her nether mound. He gave her inner thighs the same attention he had given her bosom. Eagerly, she parted her legs to grant him greater access. A musky, heady scent enveloped him. Gripping her posterior, he applied his mouth to her moist slit.

"Ahhhhhh!" Maline arched her spine and half rose off the bed, as if seeking to take flight. Subsiding, she clamped her hands on the back of his head and tried to push him up inside of her.

When Fargo's tongue found her passion knob, Maline went berserk. She thrashed and kicked and moaned loud enough to be heard in the great hall downstairs.

Fargo did not care if the whole world heard. His pole was rock hard, his body burning with the most basic of human needs. Craving release, he fought the urge for both their sakes. He licked and sucked and sucked and licked until Maline was a human volcano about to erupt. She tugged on his hair, saying over and over, "Please! Please! Please!"

At last Fargo obliged. Holding her bottom in both hands, he rose onto his knees, touched the tip of his lance to her tunnel, and rammed into her as if trying to impale her. Her head snapped back, her ruby lips parted. Her eyes widened and glazed, but only for a few seconds. Then she held onto him, grinding her hips to meet his thrusts, matching his speed, pacing herself as he was doing.

Like an orchestra rising to a crescendo of wonderful sound, so they rose to a crescendo of physical delight. Their pleasure knew no bounds. They were throbbing with the pulse of life when Maline bit his arm and looked at him with pleading eyes. He was inclined to hold off even longer, but she did something with her hips that sent a luscious shiver through his loins and shattered the mental dam that held back the sensual floodgates.

Growling deep in his throat, Fargo pounded into her. She met him with astounding strength in her supple limbs. They rocked the four-poster bed so that the posts thumped and the canopy shook in the grip of a man-made earthquake.

How long they were lost in sheer ecstasy, Fargo could not say. They surged and grappled and lunged and stroked until both reached the summit. Maline cried out first, throwing her head from side to side like a woman gone mad, her whole body the same hue as the flames in the hearth. Fargo's release left him spent. Done, he collapsed on top of her, then rolled to one side to spare her his pressing weight.

The maid chuckled. She talked softly in French, to herself. Her fingers entwined in his beard, and she pulled his face up so she could look him in the eyes. "*Merci, monsieur*," she breathed. "*Magnifique!*"

"You're welcome," Fargo said, grinning. "Any time." Nestling his cheek against her breast, he closed his eyes. After the long day he'd had, he was exhausted. He looked forward to dozing off. But try as he might, he couldn't. For minutes on end he lay there listening to Maline's rhythmic breathing and being lightly rocked by the rise and fall of her chest.

Annoyed at himself, Fargo shifted position to make himself more comfortable. He willed himself to relax. It failed to work. Instead, a pricking between his shoulder blades flared his wilderness-bred senses to full life. It was the same sensation he had felt time and again since entering Castle Conover. It was the conviction that he was being spied on.

Livid with fury, Fargo cracked his eyelids. He had taken

it for granted that they would at least have the decency not to spy on him in his bedroom. He should have known differently. That whoever it was had witnessed his lovemaking added salt to the wound.

From where he lay, Fargo could see half the room. He scanned the wall above the fireplace and the shadowed corner near the door. He studied the drapes that covered the narrow window for telltale bulges. Nowhere was there evidence of a hidden lurker. So, mumbling as might a man asleep, he rolled onto his side and let his other cheek ease onto the bed.

Now Fargo could scrutinize the rest of the bedchamber. It was not as well lit except near the lantern. Through hooded lids he surveyed every square inch. He had about decided that he was wrong when a suggestion of movement fixed his interest on a painting that hung in the middle of the wall. It was of a nobleman from long ago, perhaps one of the countess's ancestors, clad in armor. He saw nothing odd about the painting itself, but under it, close to the frame, was a crack in the wall.

Fargo pretended to snore. He moved closer to the edge of the bed, his leg sliding off as if by accident. Bracing his foot on the floor, he mumbled some more, then hurled himself at the wall like a human lightning bolt.

It worked. There was a sharp intake of breath, followed by the patter of flying feet. Fargo pressed his eyes to the crack and saw a murky form flee down a narrow secret passage. The only illumination came from a short candle the figure held, which sputtered and threatened to die.

That it was a woman was obvious. A long garment, a robe, swirled around her as she rounded a corner. A pale face glowed like a firefly, then was gone.

Fargo swore. He had not been able to recognize the profile. Yet it had to have been either the countess or the cook. They were the only other women in the castle.

Stepping back, Fargo examined the wall carefully for sign of a concealed door. The only crack was the one below the painting, where mortar had been scraped out with a sharp implement. It was barely wide enough for him to stick his fingers through. He did, on a whim, and felt a peculiar knob just under the crack on the other side. On a whim, he pressed it.

A loud series of clicks ensued. Metal gears meshed. To his astonishment, the entire center of the wall rolled to the right on recessed rollers.

Dashing to the bed, Fargo donned his gun belt and his hat. With the Colt in hand, he snatched the lantern from its niche, then moved to the opening. Inside, overhead, a complicated series of pulleys and gears explained how the door worked.

The big man advanced with all the stealth of a mountain cat. The passageway was just wide enough for a single person. Several times his wide shoulders scraped the walls. As with any wild thing that called the wide open spaces home, he had an intense dislike of being hemmed in. He had the illusion of winding his way down the gullet of a gargantuan beast.

Fargo passed two turns before he came to another room. A faint glow rimming a crack at eye level gave it away. A glance revealed Jim Conover bent over the mahogany desk in the study, scribbling his signature on document after document.

The Kansan looked tired and bitter and extremely sad, all at the same time. Setting down his quill, he stretched, then opened a drawer and took out a bottle of scotch. A few generous gulps, and he resumed work.

Fargo padded on, holding the lantern low in case anyone took a shot at him. The walls gave off a strong musty scent. In the years since the castle had been built, not much dust had accumulated—enough, though, to indicate the passage saw regular use.

Far ahead a door faintly opened and closed. A gust of cold wind seemed to waft up out of the very bowels of the earth to strike Fargo head on. It brought a foul odor, a stench so rank that Fargo would have gagged had he not covered his nose and mouth with his forearm. The odor was the stink of death, of decayed flesh and rotting organs. It made Fargo's skin creep from a legion of bumps. His imagination ran wild with images of hellish pits and creatures spawned in nightmares.

Shaking his head, Fargo got a grip on himself. He was being childish. The only dangers the castle harbored were human in guise. His Colt could deal with whatever he encountered.

Going on, Fargo went around another turn. He had a sense that the floor sloped gradually lower. Soon he came to a junction where passages branched to either side. Stumped, he paused.

If Fargo was right, he was on the first floor. The branches, he reasoned, must lead to rooms that flanked the great hall. Since he was more interested in what might lie under the castle, he proceeded straight, the floor dropping by degrees until it ended at a wide tunnel that bore to the right and the left.

With no idea what to expect, Fargo turned right. His lantern played over locked doors with small barred windows. Into each he peered, but the light did not penetrate the blackness far enough to reveal what the rooms contained.

The stench had been growing worse. Now another gust of air hit him, as if the portal far below had been opened again. The odor swamped him, choking off his breath. It was worse than the stink of a maggot-infested deer carcass, worse than that of buffalo butchered by hide hunters and left lying under the hot sun for days on end.

Swallowing bile, Fargo came to a short flight of stairs that led down. Hoisting the lantern, he discovered a broad chamber half the size of the great hall. The floor was bare of carpet. Instead of furniture, it was dotted with outlandish devices the likes of which Fargo had never seen.

One was a long table covered by upthrust razor spikes.

Another was a rack of some sort, with metal bracelets to hold wrists and ankles. Yet a third consisted of a spartan frame and ropes that could be winched apart, stretching or tearing whatever was tied to them. There were others, obscene and degraded contraptions whose vile purposes were known only to their demented designers.

But it was not the gruesome implements that horrified Fargo nearly so much as the shattered, broken, torn forms that were strapped or tied to them. Bones had been splintered, eyes gouged out, fingers chopped off. Buckskin garments had been ripped to shreds.

Enough remained for Fargo to identify the victims. The style of their hair, their moccasins, and the parfleches piled beside the steps told Fargo that those who were slain had been Ute warriors. They had been dragged to the dungeon, hideously tortured, and left to rot where they lay.

Fargo recalled the band that had come to parley with the Conovers. Disgust sickened him. The Utes had done their share of killing whites, but they had done nothing to deserve *this*. No one ever deserved to be tortured to death.

Did Jim Conover know? That was the crucial question. Somehow, Fargo could not see the Kansan resorting to such foul treatment. Yet Conover had to be aware of the hidden passages and the dungeon; he had to know about the terrible devices. Could it be that Jim Conover was a wolf in sheep's clothing? That he only acted the part of being a henpecked pawn?

Suddenly, deep in the dungeon, the darkness shifted. Fargo started, leveling his pistol. Something was back there, and it had spotted him. He backed to the doorway, letting it come to him. A few yards farther and he would see it clearly.

Without warning, the lantern went out, shrouding the dungeon and the corridor in inky gloom.

Fargo had not thought to check the kerosene. He gave the lantern a shake in frustration, then hurled it at a huge black mass that heaved out of thin air before him. He fired just as a blow slammed his right shoulder, a blow that jarred him to the bone and set his ears to ringing. He was flung back into the passageway, his right arm numb, nearly falling.

The black shape filled the doorway. Fargo fired again. A horrid screech blasted his ears, then the thing swept toward him. He fired a third time, blindly, but must have missed because the shape did not cry out and did not slow down. Sprinting backward, he turned and did what logic dictated; he ran.

Without so much as a glimmer of light to guide him, it was like being in a bottomless pit. The blackness was almost tangible. He careened off doors and walls, while behind him lumbered his huge pursuer. It had to be Quirinoc, Fargo suspected. And once the hunchback's steely fingers closed on his throat, it would be all over.

A patch of slightly lighter darkness hinted at the opening to the passageway that had brought him there. Fargo took it, and as he did, clawed fingers snagged his back but were unable to find purchase. He pumped his legs for all he was worth, his own heavy breathing mixed with the rasp of the brute on his heels.

Fargo was surprised by the hunchback's speed. Before this, Quirinoc had always plodded around like an overfed ox; now he was an agile tiger.

A troubling thought bothered Fargo as he raced around yet another bend and flew down a long, straight stretch: What if it wasn't the hunchback? He tried to dismiss the notion as silly. After all, who else could it be? But it gnawed at his mind like a dog worrying a bone who would not let go.

When his feet gained level ground, Fargo stopped and whirled. He had reached the first floor. No light filtered down the passage, but he remembered that particular spot as being wide enough to make a stand. He'd rather go down fighting than be brought low from behind. Crouching, he extended his revolver.

It took a few moments for the unnatural quiet to sink in. No lumbering tread issued from below. No grunts or heaving breaths proved that he was still being chased. The only sound was his own breathing and the pounding of his veins in his temples. Fargo sucked in air, then held it, every fiber tensed. Where was the hunchback?

From the depths of the castle carried a low, menacing rumble, such as a grizzly in its cave den might make, or an enraged buffalo that had missed a charge.

Fargo backed against a wall so no one could get at him from the rear. Beads of sweat trickled down his brow, stinging his eyes. He wiped them with his sleeve. Moments weighted with milestones dragged by, yet no one came after him. He switched the Colt to his left hand so he could wipe his palm dry.

Finally convinced that Quirinoc had given up, Fargo groped along the wall to ensure he took the correct fork. In the total darkness he often stumbled like an infant taking its first few steps. For an eternity he hiked on through the pitch black unknown with one hand always brushing the left wall.

At the next junction Fargo took what he believed to be the correct fork. Soon, however, it became clear that the inky realm had confused his usually eagle-sharp senses. He did not pass the study, as he had a while ago. Instead, a glittering yellow pinpoint guided him to a room he had not set eyes on.

It was a parlor. The carpet and furnishings were the same as elsewhere. A leather sofa was directly in line with the peephole. On that sofa reclined the Countess Arlette Leonie Mignon d'Arcy Conover and her male secretary, Albion. And she was not dictating a letter.

The raven-haired beauty wore a plush white robe, nothing else. She sat with her back against an arm, her arms and legs wide. Between her marble limbs knelt the tall albino, fully dressed. He had her left breast in his mouth and was

66

kneading the other, while she clutched his hair and raked his back.

No gentleness or tenderness marked their coupling. As Fargo looked on, Albion shifted his mouth to the lower portion of her breast and nipped it with his sharp front teeth, drawing blood. Most women would have cried out, or cuffed him. Not the countess. Throwing her head from side to side, she hissed like a serpent in the throes of mating and gave his head a jerk that would have snapped the spine of a lesser man.

"Yes, my love! Oh, yes! More! More!"

Albion gave her what she wanted, squeezing her breasts so hard that the bruises he left were visible from where Fargo stood. It drove Arlette to a peak of passion. Grasping his right hand, she thrust it under the folds of her robe, between her legs. Whatever he did caused her eyes to flutter and her body to quake.

"Oh, darling!" Arlette said, raining fiery kisses on her alabaster lover's face. "If only I hadn't had to marry that pathetic mouse! I can't stand it when he touches me. He's so weak, so puny."

Albion's response was to lever his arm up and down. The countess bent like a bow and bit her own lip to keep from crying out. Her breasts shook as she swayed like a cobra, her eyes smoldering with primitive lust.

"Soon," Arlette husked. "Very soon."

Fargo was wondering what she meant by that when the door to the parlor resounded to loud thumps. Her husband's shout stiffened her and her paramour.

"Arlette, dearest? Are you in there?"

"One moment!" the countess replied, smoothing her robe as Albion darted to a far corner and ducked behind a chair. She rose when he was safely hidden. Throwing a bolt, she regarded Conover with displeasure. "Are you finished signing everything already?"

Jim nodded and entered. He gazed suspiciously around, but when he saw no one else, he relaxed and clasped her arm. "I hurried so we could spend some time together before you retire. It's been ages since you favored me with a visit to my bedroom."

Fargo blinked. They were husband and wife, and they had *separate* bedrooms?

Arlette frowned. "Not tonight, darling. I have an awful headache."

"Not another one?"

The countess shrugged. "What can I say? I told you when we met that my family has a history of severe headaches. There's nothing I can do about it." She glanced at the corner where the albino was crouched, then perked up, saying, "But I'll tell you what. Why don't we go down to the kitchen and have Beverly fix us some coffee and cakes? I wouldn't mind a snack before we turn in."

"Very well," Jim said, resigned. They departed, and the moment the door closed, Albion rose and hurried across the room. But not in the direction of the door. No, he came straight toward the peephole—and Fargo's hiding place.

6

Skye Fargo made no attempt to hide. He did not run off as he had in the dungeon. Lowering his hand to his Colt, he prepared to leap out once the albino opened the hidden door. But at the very last instant, as Albion reached out to touch a spot on the wall below the peephole, the secretary paused, pondered a moment, then turned and went out the same way the Conovers had.

Fargo bent to examine the wall. There had to be a means of opening the hidden door, but he could not find it. Foiled, he continued down the secret passageway, seeking a way out.

Before long he came to another chamber. This time it was not a glimmer of light that brought him to a stop. It was the sound of someone weeping. Checking, he discovered another peephole and peered into a bedchamber much like his own. No lantern glowed, but a tiny fire ate at logs in the fireplace, casting just enough illumination to reveal the miserable figure lying on the big bed.

Beverly Shannon wore a few underthings, nothing else. She was incredibly beautiful, her smooth skin glistening in the flickering firelight. Her ample bosom, partially freed, swelled like ripe watermelons. Magnificent thighs tapered to dainty feet with painted toenails. Her sandy hair resembled a burnished bronze helmet. She had her face buried in her pillow and was crying softly.

Fargo felt it wrong to intrude on her private moment. He shifted to leave, then stopping when a harsh knock sounded and Arlette Conover called, "Miss Shannon, we require your services!"

Beverly sat up, as white as a sheet. "Just a moment!" she blurted. Dashing to a chair over which she had thrown her uniform, she quickly shrugged into it, then stepped to a mirror.

"Hurry it up," the countess demanded.

"Coming!" Beverly fussed with her hair, wiped her face, using the corner of the bed quilt, and admitted her caller. "Sorry it took me so long. I was ready to turn in."

Arlette stalked into the bedchamber and placed her hands on her hips. "My husband and I require coffee and cakes. You will accommodate us, of course."

"Of course," Beverly said. She started to slip past, but the countess seized her arm and roughly pushed her back against the wall.

"Not so fast," Arlette Conover snapped. "You have some explaining to do."

"I do?"

Arlette gave Beverly a shake. "Don't be coy with me, wench! Albion told me what you have been up to. How you've been sneaking about the castle eavesdropping on conversations—"

"But I wasn't!" Beverly interrupted, and was shaken twice as hard for her impertinence.

"Don't lie, bitch!" Arlette's face was a twisted mask of savage hatred. "How much did you overhear when Albion and I were in the drawing room?"

"Nothing! Not a word!"

The countess's eyes were snakish slits. "Albion doesn't believe you, and neither do I." She leaned closer, pressing her red nails against Shannon's cheek. "For your own sake, you had better be telling the truth. I never have liked you. If you're not careful, you might end up vanishing off the face of the earth, just as those Utes and Jasper Flint did."

Terror made Beverly cringe. "I know nothing!" she

wailed, shoving her tormentor from her. Sobbing, she flew from the chamber, the patter of her footsteps receding.

Arlette Conover grinned, then threw back her head and cackled. Her mirth was sadistic, jarring, elemental, an expression of pure soulless evil. Still cackling, she sashayed out the door.

It gave Fargo much food for thought as he traveled on to a junction that took a fork that brought him to the second floor. Finding his own room proved easy after that.

Maline still slept soundly, curled into a ball, her features angelic.

Closing the secret door was not enough. Fargo hiked his right leg and slid his Arkansas toothpick from its ankle sheath in his right boot. Next he cut five whangs from his buckskin shirt and wedged them into the crack.

Bolting the door, Fargo sat on the bed. He should undress, but he was so tired that he simply flopped onto his back, rested a hand on the maid's golden breasts, and promptly drifted into dreamland. Not surprisingly, he had a nightmare in which he was chased down an unending black passageway by a monstrous creature that had heaved up out of the depths of the earth. In his nightmare he ran and ran and ran, the creature's bloody talons poised to rip and rend should he stumble.

And he did.

An hour before sunrise the Trailsman was up and dashing water on his face from the wash basin. He did not need to be awakened by a clock or someone else, as slothful city dwellers did. For years he had been getting up at the crack of dawn, and sooner. Now it was a habit.

Maline Bonacieux had left sometime in the middle of the night. A small note on the pillow read, "*Merci*. Another time, perhaps?" He crumpled the paper and stuffed it into a pocket.

Castle Conover was as silent as a tomb. Fargo strode to the landing, his spurs jangling. He did not expect anyone else to be roaming the halls quite yet, so he was surprised when he descended the stairs and ran into Beverly Shannon, just coming out of the corridor that led to her bedroom. "Morning," he said.

Beverly had been staring absently at the floor. Startled, she looked up. "Oh! Skye!" Oddly, she blushed a deep scarlet, then averted her face. "Good morning."

"Are you always up this early?" Fargo asked to make small talk, falling into step beside her.

"Except on my two days off a month, yes. The countess insists that she be served breakfast in bed promptly at six, and it takes a while to get the stove fired up and all."

"You only get two days to yourself each month?"

Beverly acted more interested in the wall than in him. "If she had her way, none of the staff would have a single day off. Jim wouldn't hear of it, of course. So she gave in."

Shannon's personal affairs were none of Fargo's business, but after seeing her cry her heart out, he could not keep quiet. "I know Jim and you are friends. But if it was me, I wouldn't put up with how the countess treats you. I'd pack my bags and leave."

A sigh of yearning escaped her. "I wish to God I could. I truly do."

"What's holding you here?"

Beverly glanced at him. She was on the verge of saying something. But just then they passed a darkened corridor, and from it came a rustling noise that widened her eyes in fright. "I told you," she said much more loudly than was necessary. "I stay because the pay is good. Now, if you'll excuse me." She ran off, her head bent in misery.

As much as he would have liked to, Fargo did not go after her. He had to be long gone before sunup. To that end, recalling directions Jim had given him during supper, he walked the length of the great hall to an enormous pair of wooden doors. They opened onto a small courtyard. Beyond was the portcullis.

At the southwest corner horses milled in a corral, their

breath puffing from icy nostrils. Cold knifed into Fargo as he walked to the stone stable and into the first room on the right, where the tack was stored. Picking a saddle blanket and saddle, he returned to the corral, draped them over the top rail, and took hold of the gate to swing it open.

"What in hell do you reckon you're doin', mister?"

In the stable entrance stood a burly, unkempt man in jeans he had hastily pulled on over his long underwear. His pants were hitched up above his ankles and his belt unbuckled. He looked comical. There was nothing comical, however, about the scattergun he leveled.

"You must be Cass," Fargo said.

The stable man nodded. "And you must be the feller who showed up here yesterday on foot. Now I catch you tryin' to sneak off with one of our horses. I'd be in my rights to blow you in half."

Fargo made no sudden moves. At that range, the man could not possibly miss. "Talk to Conover. He gave his permission."

Cass snorted. "You want me to go into the castle? Hell, mister, you must be plumb loco. I *never* go in there." He jabbed an elbow at the straw-littered aisle that ran the length of the stable. "I have me a room at the back, and that's where I stay when I'm not busy tendin' stock. Even have that English jasper or that blond filly fetch me my meals, so I don't ever need to go past the courtyard."

"Why?" Fargo quizzed him.

Cass might have answered, but Jim Conover picked that moment to bustle outdoors with another man dogging him. Conover was bundled in a heavy sheepskin coat and a fur hat. "Good morning, gentlemen," he greeted them, then saw the scattergun. "Hold on. What's the meaning of this, Cass?"

The stable man lowered the barrel. "I heard someone out here and came for a look-see."

Conover walked up to Fargo. "There's no need to be

73

pointing guns at our guest. He's going after the Utes who stole his stallion."

"By his lonesome?" Cass asked, snickering when the silver baron nodded. "I reckon we won't be seein' each other again, then, mister," he said to Fargo, and walked off.

"Forgive his manners," Jim said. "He's rough around the edges, but he knows horses." He winked. "Besides, he was one of the few men willing to come way out here to work for us."

Enough precious time had already been wasted. Fargo opened the gate, selected a dun that showed promise of stamina and speed, and threw on the blanket and saddle. As he worked, Conover and the other man entered the corral.

"By the way, Skye, this is Robert Cheeves, our butler. My wife brought him with her, but don't hold that against him. He's pretty decent for a Brit."

The Englishman was in his late fifties or early sixties. Balding, he had a hook nose rimmed by owlish sorrowful eyes. "Morning, governor," he said in an accent thick enough to cut with a Bowie. "On my oath, it takes a lot of gumption to go traipsing after those red devils on your own."

Fargo grunted. He was busy cinching up, then marked the pale tinge of pink that banded the eastern horizon. "If I'm not back by sunset, don't send anyone after me," he told Conover. "There will be no need."

The Kansan scowled. "I wish you'd let one or two of us go with you. Quirinoc, at least. I haven't seen him yet today, but I'm sure I can rustle him up in short order."

Fargo wondered if the hunchback's absence meant the brute had been hurt the night before. He reminded himself that he had no proof it had been Quirinoc who attacked him in the dungeon. But who else could it have been?

Leading the dun from the corral, Fargo closed the gate and forked leather. "If someone will let me out, I'd be obliged," he said.

Jim Conover offered his hand. He shook with sincere

warmth. "Take care of yourself, friend. When you get back, we'll drink to your success."

"You're on," Fargo promised.

The baron and the butler worked the chain themselves, grinding the portcullis slowly upward. Fargo bent to pass beneath the wicked spiked bars, straightened, and waved as he pricked his spurs into the dun.

Snow, snow everywhere. A thin crust had formed; the dun's hooves crunched with every step. In the false gray light of predawn the Rocky Mountains were lifeless and still, as if holding their breath in anticipation of dawn. Mule deer scattered into the trees as Fargo rode to the southeast at a gallop. He had time and distance to make up.

Within minutes Fargo struck the trail left by the band. Thanks to the icy sheen, the tracks were now clearly defined. At a trot he paralleled them for the better part of an hour. The eastern sky gradually brightened from dull gray to bright gray to a pale suggestion of rosy gold.

He hoped he had not been wrong about the Utes making camp early the night before. If they had gone any distance and were already on their way south, it would be next to impossible to catch them before another day was done.

Apparently the dun had not been exercised in some time. Mile after mile fell behind them, yet it showed no fatigue.

A chorus of birds heralded the rising of the sun. With full daylight, Fargo moved more cautiously. He never advanced into open spaces without first scouring the terrain ahead. Approximately forty minutes after the sun came up, he came on the Ute camp. A wide area where the snow had been cleared so the horses could graze contained the Ovaro's prints. The embers of the fire were still warm, which was encouraging.

Pushing on, Fargo rode until the middle of the morning. He was gaining, but not fast enough to suit him. On a wooded ridge he rested the dun. From then until noon he did not slacken the pace once.

The Utes were in a hurry and showed no sign of stopping

anytime soon. Since they could not possibly know that someone was after them, there had to be another reason for their haste. Maybe, Fargo mused, they wanted to get shy of the castle and its vicinity. Given what had happened to their friends, he couldn't blame them.

It must have been one o'clock when Fargo spied stick figures in the distance. Seeking heavier cover, he doubled his pace until the figures grew in size to take on the aspect of mounted men. He had done it.

The five Utes were heavily armed, strung out in single file. A tall warrior at the head of the line was leading the Ovaro by a rope made of buffalo hide. They had slowed a little now that the castle was far behind them. As Indians always did when in hostile country, they traveled in silence, on the alert.

Fargo hung a quarter of a mile back, in the pines. He could have swung wide and gone on ahead to ambush them. But he had been serious about recovering the stallion without bloodshed.

The Utes had done him no personal wrong. Oh, they had taken his horse, but it was not as if they had stolen it out from under his very nose. They had found the pinto wandering riderless and done what anyone else would have done.

Fargo had no illusions about the outcome should he ride right up to them to ask for the Ovaro back. The warriors were not about to part with their prize unless it was for something of equal value, and he had nothing to trade.

The afternoon waxed and waned. Fargo saw no opportunity to retake the stallion before nightfall. As the shadows lengthened, the Utes cast about for a spot to camp, selecting a gully that would shield them from the wind and was largely bare of snow. Two of them kindled a fire while two more walked off with their bows in hand. The fifth took care of the horses.

From a dense stand over a hundred yards away, Fargo saw when the hunters returned bearing a doe they swiftly butchered and roasted. He was upwind, but the sight of them tearing into the dripping brown meat with their white teeth and wolfing great chunks set his stomach to growling fiercely.

After their meal the Utes settled down around their small fire to swap tales and laughter until close to midnight. Fargo huddled under cover, his arms clasped to his shoulders, stamping his feet now and then to ward off frostbite.

The tall warrior was the last to turn in. He rose and checked their tethered horses, then lay close to the fire covered by Fargo's blankets, his head resting on Fargo's saddle, Fargo's Henry rifle tucked to his side.

One o'clock came and went. Convinced they were sound asleep, Fargo crept from his hiding place, palming his Colt. The dun was tied to a tree and would be safe until he came back for it.

One of the Utes snored loudly. The fire had dwindled to tiny flames that gave off tendrils of white smoke. Fargo slowly approached the gully, placing each foot down carefully. Twice the crust crackled. He feared it would bring the band to their feet bristling with weapons, but neither noise was loud enough to rouse them.

A phantom made real, Fargo stole into the gully and was fifteen feet from the circle of sleeping bodies when the shortest Ute rolled over, facing him, and mumbled in his sleep. Fargo watched the man's eyes. When they did not open, he circled around to the far side, where the tall warrior lay.

Now came the hard part. Fargo was not about to ride off without his belongings. He didn't own much in the way of worldly goods, but they were all he had. He sneaked to within an arm's length of the sleeping Ute, bent his elbow, and was all set to bash the man over the head just hard enough to knock him out when a horrendous racket broke out to the north, at the spot where he had left the dun. The animal commenced neighing in panic and pain and stomping its hooves as if it were being attacked by a predator, although no roars or snarls rent the night.

The Utes leaped to their feet, automatically facing the commotion, which put their backs to Fargo. The whinnies rose to an anguished pinnacle, the brush around the dun shaking and bending as it would if a grizzly were in there. The tall Ute started to turn toward their own mounts and found himself looking down the barrel of Fargo's cocked Colt.

Fargo put a finger to his lips. Baffled fury blazed in the tall warrior's dark eyes, but he stood stock still while Fargo snatched the Henry and backed up several steps.

His broad contact with dozens of tribes had given Fargo fluency in several tongues and more than a passing familiarity with a dozen others. The Ute language was not one he knew well, but he knew it well enough to call out, "Drop your weapons!"

The other three turned, or began to. When they saw they were covered, two of them did as he had directed. The third, the short warrior, hesitated, torn between following their example and using the lance he held. A single word from the tall Ute persuaded him to cast the lance and a sheath knife to the ground.

So far, so good, Fargo reflected. The uproar to the north had died. But if a grizzly was on the prowl, it might show up at any moment. Fargo motioned for the Utes to move to the west of the fire, signaling they should halt twenty feet out with their arms upraised. They complied, but none of them liked it.

Keeping one eye on them and one on the rim of the gully, Fargo retrieved his saddle blanket and draped it over the Ovaro. The stallion acted glad to see him, nuzzling him repeatedly as he saddled up and drew the cinch tight.

The Utes made no move to stop him. Fargo noticed that the tall one appeared to be puzzled. Touching the pinto, Fargo said in their tongue, "My horse."

The warriors exchanged glances. One whispered. The

tall one raised his head and said in atrocious broken English, "We not savvy, white man. Why you not kill us?"

"I only want what is mine," Fargo responded in the same language.

The warrior considered this as Fargo hastily gathered his saddlebags and bedroll. "Are you from the stone lodge?"

"The castle, you mean?" Fargo said. "No, I'm passing through. But I stayed there last night after my horse ran away during the snowstorm."

Excitedly, the tall warrior translated. A flurry of comments resulted in the tall Ute saying, "You stayed in stone lodge? Yet man-beast not kill you?"

Fargo paused. "What are you talking about?"

The Ute made a remark in his own tongue that Fargo did not quite catch. Then, in English, the warrior said, "We call him Evil That Walks Like Man. With my own eyes I saw him crush warriors with bare hands. We shoot arrows, it not hurt him. We stab with knives, him not stop. Bad medicine, this one."

Did they mean the hunchback? Fargo wanted to learn more, but the short warrior wore an edgy look, as though the man was just waiting for a chance to jump him. It was best to light a shuck while he still could. Accordingly, he stepped into the stirrups and reined around, but did not ride off, just yet.

"If I leave your horses, I want your word that none of you will come after me," Fargo said to the tall one.

The Ute's brow creased. "You, a white man, would take word of those you call red men?"

"It's not the color of man's skin that counts, it's what is under it," Fargo countered. "So do I have your promise? I'd rather not leave you on foot so far from your village, but I don't want an arrow in my back, either."

Heated palaver among the four resulted in the tall warrior saying, "I, White Eagle, promise. My friends not go after you."

"That'll do," Fargo said, then rode off without a backward glance. To do so would be taken as a sign he had spoken with two tongues or was afraid. Once out of the gully, he trotted into the trees where the dun should be.

It was there, all right, but its heaving sides and trembling flanks were streaked with scarlet from a score of jagged wounds. Lying at its feet was the cause, a long branch that tapered to a bloody tip. Someone had deliberately poked the poor animal again and again, then left the limb lying there and gone off.

Fargo levered a round into the Henry. Rising in the stirrups, he scoured the forest. He was so intent on the surrounding undergrowth that he almost overlooked a set of tracks that ringed the stricken dun. When he did, his gut balled into a knot and his grip on the repeating rifle firmed.

Each was four times the size of a normal man's print. Whatever made them had not worn footwear, and clearly etched in the snow was telltale evidence that each foot had *three splayed toes.*

7

Skye Fargo was widely considered to be one of the best trackers alive. At one time or another he had tracked every animal on the North American continent. He could take one look at a print and tell what made it, how long ago, and even how fast the animal had been traveling at the time. Spoor was an open book to him. From grizzlies to mice, he knew them all.

So it was a profound shock for Fargo to discover a set of prints unlike any he had ever seen. Indeed, unlike any known to exist.

The shock was doubled when Fargo realized that whatever had poked the dun had done so on purpose. The culprit had wanted the horse to make a lot of noise so the racket would wake up the Utes and they would see Fargo in their camp. The culprit had wanted Fargo dead.

At that instant another tremendous uproar broke out, this time from the gully Fargo had quitted a minute ago. Screams and bellows from the Utes mingled with the squeals of terrified horses.

Fargo could not quite say what made him do what he did next. He was under no obligation to the Utes. They had let him ride off alive only because he extracted a pledge of safety at gunpoint. Yet he never hesitated. As the awful din rose to a fevered pitch, he reined the Ovaro to the south and used his spurs.

In moments the stallion burst from the heavy cover. A hundred yards it had to cover, and it did so with mane and tail flying. Fargo straightened and pressed the Henry to his shoulder, but there was nothing to shoot at. A lone body was sprawled partly in the fire, another at the gully's rim. Past them was a bulkier form twisted at an unnatural angle.

Hauling on the reins, Fargo took in the carnage. The dead man being devoured by growing flames was the short Ute. Something had smashed the warrior's face to a pulp. On the rim lay another warrior whose right arm had been snapped so brutally that bone jutted from flesh. In addition the man's throat had been torn out.

Fargo shot on by, past a dead horse whose head was tilted skyward. It had been wrenched so far back over the animal's shoulders that it had almost been torn off.

From above the west rim rose more screaming and nickering and the crash of undergrowth.

Bending forward, Fargo took the slope at full gallop. As he cleared the crest, he found another Ute in his path. At least the body was, at any rate. The head was five feet away, upright, blank eyes fixed forever in an expression of consuming fear.

The only creature Fargo knew of strong enough to rip heads from bodies was a grizzly. But no grizzly ever born left three-toed tracks.

From the forest rose the clash of conflict. The last two Utes were engaged in a fighting retreat, trying to escape whatever had slain their companions. Fargo came upon another horse. This one had its skull caved in, the blood and brains oozing freely from the shattered cavity.

Into the trees Fargo raced. Up ahead figures moved. In the darkness they were vague outlines, but he could tell that two of them were men. That another was a horse was likewise apparent. The last shape, though, was twice as tall as the warriors and half as wide as the horse. It was, in fact, the size of the hunchback, but it moved faster than the hunchback ever had, darting from point to point with the speed of a striking rattler.

Even as Fargo set eyes on the bedlam, the hulking creature seized one of the Utes, swept the man overhead, and dashed him onto a log. Sixty feet away Fargo heard the crack, snap, and pop of breaking bones.

Taking a gamble that he would not hit the surviving warrior, Fargo banged off two swift shots. They had no effect.

In an inexorable rush the brute closed on the lone Ute, whose height revealed him to be White Eagle. The warrior stood his ground, a knife uplifted. Fargo saw their shapes blend and blur, saw the dull gleam of the falling blade.

It availed the Ute little. The living nightmare gripped an arm in each giant hand. With a mighty heave the thing tore the limbs from their sockets and threw them aside.

Fargo fired twice more. At the second shot the nightmare stiffened, then wheeled and melted into the vegetation. Fargo could not have been thirty feet from it, yet when he reached the same spot, the thing was nowhere to be seen.

A groan stopped Fargo from plunging into the woods. White Eagle was still alive, but the amount of blood he had lost meant he would not be alive very much longer. Jumping off the pinto, Fargo sank to his right knee and lifted the Ute's head onto his leg. He did not care that blood soaked his pant leg and covered half his boot.

The tall warrior's eyes fluttered. Opening with a snap, they mirrored anguish beyond human endurance. White Eagle gazed wildly at the star-speckled heavens, then focused on Fargo. "Flee!" he said in his own tongue. "Save yourself!"

"What did this?" Fargo asked urgently.

White Eagle had trouble answering. His lips quivered, his eyes were already glazing. "Evil That Walks Like Man," he said. Convulsing, he cried out in his own language, and died.

Fargo slowly rose. Other than the wheezing of a nearby Ute mount, the pristine woodland was deceptively peaceful. Whatever had rampaged among the Utes was gone. He could feel it. Which added to the mystery. Why had it gone after the Indians, but not after him? Was it afraid of his guns?

An hour later Fargo rode off, after he had dragged the bodies into the gully and covered them with as many rocks and branches as he could find to deter scavengers.

All except one. Fargo wrapped the tall warrior in a blanket and draped him over the back of the Ute mount that had not run off. By tying the wrists to the ankles under the animal's belly, Fargo ensured the body would stay on until the horse reached the Ute village. A sharp smack sent the mount trotting southward.

Fargo watched until it faded in the distance. Wearily forking leather, he collected the dun and headed north. He needed rest, but he would rather put as much distance as he could between the gully and him by daybreak.

Sticking to open tracts, the Henry resting across his lap, Fargo held to a brisk walk until a yellow crown framed the eastern horizon. He had a long way to go to reach the castle. Too long, in his condition.

In a secluded cottonwood grove watered by a stream, Fargo spread out his bedroll. In the back of his mind was the nagging worry that whatever had wiped out the Utes might sneak up on him while he slept. But he had seen no sign of it, nor its tracks. His need of rest outweighed the risk. A few hours slumber and he would be raring to go. Plus he had the dun to think of. It was stiff and sore and half worn out.

A bright beam of sunshine full on his face woke Fargo when the sun was directly overhead. He lost no time in saddling up and moving on. From his saddlebags he treated himself to jerky and pemmican.

The day was uneventful. Sunset came and went and still Fargo rode on. When the squat, toadlike silhouette of the castle loomed before him, the stars had been out for hours. Light framed a score of windows. From one of them wafted the sound of someone crying.

Fargo reined up at the portcullis. He had to yell several

times before Cass shambled out of the darkness, scattergun in hand.

"Damnation! It's you! I never figured to set eyes on you again."

"Open up," Fargo said.

The stable man leaned his shotgun against the wall. Gripping the spokes of the wheel that worked the chain, he cranked the heavy gate upward. He was sweating and puffing when at last he raised it high enough for Fargo to pass under.

In the courtyard the crying was louder. Dismounting, Fargo handed the reins to Cass and nodded at a window high above them. "What's going on?"

"That must be the cook. She's taken Conover's death real hard. Fainted, she did, when they brought the body in this evenin'."

A hot knife twisted Fargo's insides. "Jim Conover is *dead*?"

Cass nodded. "Killed by Utes. It happened late in the afternoon, after he went out again." The stable man paused. "Conover was real worried about you. Every hour or so he'd ride around the castle a few times, hopin' to spot you on your way back. The last time, about four, I was shoein' a horse when I heard this godawful screech off to the west, in the trees. I hollered to Mrs. Conover, and she sent that white freak and me off to find her husband."

"Did you see the Utes with your own eyes?"

"Not exactly, no. But the albino said he did. And you should take a gander at the body." Motioning, Cass walked toward the stable. "They left it in here. The missus didn't want it stinkin' up her precious castle, I reckon." He moved down the center aisle, taking a lantern from a peg. "'Course, it don't smell much yet, but it will by tomorrow. It's one of the worst I've ever come across."

In a small, dusty stone room past the last stall on the cold floor, a blanket had been placed over the body of the erstwhile lord of Castle Conover. Squatting, Fargo peeled the top of the blanket high enough to look under.

Jim Conover had been butchered. There was no other word for it. His torso had been hacked and cut and slashed to ribbons. His clothes and flesh hung in strips. The inner organs were exposed, a loop of intestine drooping through a slit in his abdomen. Oddly, his head and limbs had not been touched. His features were frozen in the horror that had overcome him during his last moments.

"See?" Cass said. "Ain't no doubt about it. Had to be Utes. Them and their damned tomahawks. They chopped the poor man to pieces."

Fargo made no comment. The fire that burned within him changed to brittle ice. His jaw muscles hardened, and his hands clenched around the Henry until the knuckles were pale.

"The missus plans to send me into Idaho Springs in the mornin'. Says we have to get word to their lawyer in Denver. Somethin' about all Jim's assets being turned over to her, or some such legal nonsense."

"She isn't wasting any time," Fargo said under his breath.

"What was that, hoss? I didn't quite catch it."

"Nothing." Fargo gently lowered the blanket and walked out. "Will you make sure my stallion and the dun are rubbed down and fed. I'd be grateful."

Cass shrugged. "That's what I'm here for. Though, now that Mr. Conover is gone, the missus will likely send me packin'. She never did cotton to me." He swore. "Why, the first day I came here, the very first day, that woman tried to boss me around. Told me I had to take a bath regular like and wash my clothes once a week. Can you imagine her gall!"

Fargo was thinking of the misguided man in the cold stable, the devoted husband who had adored the countess with his whole heart and soul. The icy sensation spread.

The stable man snickered. "I made it plain that I don't

take a bath but once a year. Hell, everyone knows that too much washin' is bad for the health. Makes you puny and sickly. But try tellin' that to those know-it-all Eur-o-peeeans."

Cass stopped at the corral. Fargo crossed to the immense double doors and entered the main hall. Here the sobs echoed and reechoed off the high walls, so that it seemed as if a throng of mourners were present. His boots slapped the stone floor crisply as he made for the stairs.

Voices coming from the corridor that linked the hall to the dining room bent his steps to the left. Someone laughed, and he was sure it must be Arlette Conover.

The raven-haired beauty was not alone. Albion sat at her elbow, the two of them eating cheese and bread and sipping red wine from crystal goblets. Their arms brushed, their noses nearly touched. Grinning from ear to ear, they did not realize Fargo was there until he tapped the Henry's barrel on the wall.

The albino started and began to rise, but the countess gripped his wrist. She was not the least bit flustered. As calm as you please, she plucked a small triangle of yellow cheese from a silver plate and took a lingering bite. "Well, well, well. Mr. Fargo. You made it back safe and sound. Thank goodness."

Fargo moved to the table. "I see you're in mourning for your husband."

Arlette's eyes flashed spite she quickly quelled. "We each show grief in our own manner. For my part, I have never been one to moan and groan and bawl myself silly. But believe me, inwardly I shed tears every minute."

The woman never knew how close she came to having the butt stock of a rifle smashed against her red lips. Cradling the Henry, Fargo turned to the albino. "Cass tells me that you saw the Utes who did it."

"Indeed," Albion said in his cultured, resonant voice. "We were searching the forest for Lord Conover when I spotted a pack of them riding off."

"How many were there?"

"Oh, seven or eight. I couldn't be certain. They were on horseback and moving fast. Painted devils, with feathers in their hair and bloody tomahawks in their hands. I knew the moment I saw them that something dreadful had occurred."

Adopting a poker face, Fargo said, "*All* of them had tomahawks?"

"As near as I could determine," Albion said. "But, again, it was difficult to be sure with so many trees in the way. Shortly after that, I found the body and yelled for the stable man. If we hadn't drifted apart, he would have seen the Utes, too."

Any faint doubts Fargo held evaporated in the furnace of rising outrage. He knew who had killed Jim Conover—and it had not been Utes. He also had a fair suspicion why, but he lacked proof. "Where was Quirinoc while all this was going on?"

Arlette replied. "Oh, he was with me. Why do you ask? Surely, you don't think he did it?"

"No," Fargo admitted. "I'm just curious whether he left the castle yesterday and might not have gotten back until sometime late today."

"Where would he go?" Arlette asked. "No, Quirinoc has been here ever since you left. I can vouch for that personally." She stretched languidly, like a sleek cat in need of exercise. "As for you, Mr. Fargo, you're more than welcome to stay the night. Perhaps you would see fit to go with Mr. Cass to the settlements tomorrow and let the authorities know about the Utes who stole your horse."

The woman should be an actress, Fargo mused sourly. "The warriors who stole my horse are all dead."

Arlette Conover took the news without a shred of surprise. "Every last one? Pity. The authorities might have wanted to question them about the identities of those who murdered my husband."

Fargo pivoted before he gave himself away. Striding to the doorway, he halted when the countess said his name.

"James doesn't have many close friends. I know he thought highly of you. Perhaps you would see fit to come back in a few days for the funeral. I'm having him buried on that little rise west of here so I can see his gravestone from my window. It will be a constant reminder of his love."

The smart thing to do was stay on her good side, so Fargo responded, "I'd be honored. Your husband was a decent man. It's too bad that he let himself get killed the way he did. Sometimes we're blind to what is going on around us."

Arlette's eyes narrowed, and Fargo wondered if he had made a mistake. Her silken smile convinced him that she had not caught his double meaning. "How very true. Those wretched savages must have sneaked up on him like ghosts. He was never much of a woodsman, you know."

Excusing himself, Fargo retraced his steps to the great hall. The tinkle of subdued laughter mocked him as far as the tapestry. Instead of taking the stairs to his own room, Fargo veered into the corridor that soon brought him to the cook's. The door hung halfway open. From inside spilled the heartfelt sobs of the one person on earth who would lament Conover's passing for years to come.

At Fargo's light knock the sobs choked off. Beverly Shannon called out timidly, "Who is it?" When he told her, the door was flung wide. Before he could so much as lift a finger, she was in his arms, hugging him close, her face buried against his chest, her whole body quaking.

Fargo was taken aback. Putting an arm over her shoulders, he steered her into the chamber and closed the door. She cried and cried, soaking the front of his shirt. At length she stood back, sniffling, and dabbed her eyes with a handkerchief.

"I'm sorry, Skye. I had no business doing that. We hardly know each other."

"We both liked Jim," Fargo reminded her, which provoked another deluge. He moved to the bed and sat on the edge, waiting patiently while she cried herself dry on his shoulder. Only after she rested quietly against him did he bring up the reason he had paid her a visit. "I need your help. There are a few things I need to learn."

"Anything. And in return, I have a favor to ask of you."

Fargo shifted so they faced one another. "When was the last time you saw Quirinoc?"

Beverly had to think a moment. "I can't be sure. Yesterday, maybe. Or the day before. Is it important?"

It was, but Fargo pressed on. "Where were you when you heard about Jim?"

"In the kitchen, preparing supper. I'd been outside less than half an hour before that, gathering wood. And I didn't see hide nor hair of any Utes."

"Where was the countess?"

"Upstairs in her bedroom, I think. Or so Maline mentioned." Beverly wrung her hands. "The poor dear. Maline is taking this almost as hard as I am. Jim always treated her fairly and kindly."

"What about the butler, Cheeves?"

Shannon was puzzled. "What about him? He's hardly ever around. Just between you and me, the man is a lush—a lazy lush. He spends most of his time hiding so he can avoid doing work. I haven't seen him since yesterday morning at breakfast." She elaborated. "The countess insists that all the servants must eat in a small room off the kitchen. But she does allow us to take trays to our bedrooms."

Beverly paused. Fargo had the impression that she was on the verge of saying something important. But she bit her lower lip and looked away, tears flowing again. Deciding to leave her alone with her grief, he stood.

Her hand clasped his, her palm warm and soft, their fingers entwining. "Where are you going?" she asked anxiously, trying in vain to stifle the flood.

"We'll talk once you're feeling better," Fargo said.

"I don't want to be left alone."

"If you need me, just holler." It had suddenly dawned on Fargo that an urgent task needed doing, before the countess and Albion were done with their meal. Prying her hand loose, he hurried to the door. She trailed him like a forlorn puppy, choking back more sobs.

"Be careful, Skye. You have no idea what is going on around here. Nothing is as it seems."

Fargo had learned that much within five minutes of meeting the countess. Rather than dawdle to swap information, he patted Beverly's shoulder and was halfway out the door when he paused himself. "Do you have a weapon?"

Beverly shook her head, sniffling, the handkerchief over her nose. "I had no reason to think I would need one. But I can get a knife from the kitchen if need be."

That would not do, Fargo observed. To get there, she had to go downstairs and wind along a dark maze of halls. Pulling the toothpick from its ankle sheath, he reversed his grip and held the knife out, hilt first. "Take this. Don't go anywhere without it. I'll try to find a gun for you as soon as I can."

Gingerly, Beverly accepted the blade. "I appreciate your concern, but I've never hurt anyone in my entire life. I don't know if I could, even if they were trying to kill me."

Fresh in Fargo's memory was how feebly she had fought back when Albion had her in his grip. It was disturbing. He never had understood how people could allow themselves to be slaughtered as meekly as a little lamb. When his time came, he planned to fight to the last. So long as breath remained, he would resist, tooth and nail.

To Beverly Fargo said, "It's your choice. But why throw your life away? I doubt Jim would have wanted you to." Leaving her with that nugget of common sense to mull over, he hastened to the stairs and up them to the second floor. The study door was shut, but opened when he tried the latch. On the desk stood the stack of documents Arlette had insisted her husband sign.

About to enter, Fargo heard the patter of footsteps climbing the stairs. Thinking that it might be the countess or her secretary, he darted to his own room and slid inside before anyone spotted him. An ear pressed to the panel, he listened to someone approach. Whoever it was passed the study and stopped in front of his bedchamber.

Fargo heard heavy breathing. Was it the hunchback? He nearly jumped when a fist thumped heavily on the oak. Opening, he was mildly annoyed to find Beverly Shannon, his throwing knife at her side. "What's wrong?"

"You ran off so fast that I forgot to ask my favor."

"Anything. What is it?"

"You'll be leaving soon, I should think." Beverly took a deep breath. "I want you to take me along when you go."

8

"That's all?" Skye Fargo said, wishing she had stayed in her room. She did not realize it, but she had picked the wrong moment to show up. It was crucial he slip into the study while he had the chance. "Consider it done," he said, trying to brush by.

"I should warn you," Beverly said. "It might not be that simple. Arlette might not let me go."

"This is America," Fargo reminded her while checking the corridor. "No one has the right to force someone else to do anything against their will. If you want to go, I'm taking you out. And there isn't a damn thing the countess can do." Putting a hand on Beverly's shoulder, he ushered her into his bedroom. "I have no time to explain, but I want you to stay here until I get back. I won't be long."

Beverly looked so scared that Fargo shoved the Henry into her arms. "Take this, too. There's a round in the chamber. All you have to do is pull back the hammer and squeeze the trigger."

Thankfully, she did not argue. Fargo closed the door and hurried to the study. He left the study door open a few inches as a precaution. Dashing to the desk, he began sorting through the stack of documents, one by one. Some were payment vouchers for workers at the Conover mine. Others were purchase authorizations for equipment and supplies. Still others were ordinary business reports that required the Kansan's signature. Routine stuff. No wonder Jim had been bored.

Then Fargo came to the middle of the stack. It was where Albion had slipped a particular document, one bearing a red mark in a lower corner.

Fargo found it easily enough. The mark was a fancy notary public's seal. It meant the document had been notarized to prove all the signatures were authentic *before* Jim added his, which was illegal.

Quickly, he scanned the text. It was a lot of complicated lawyer talk, with fifteen-syllable words. But the gist of it was that all the assets of James Thaddeus Conover were legally handed over to his wife in the event of Jim's death.

Had Jim realized what he was signing? Fargo remembered how secretive the secretary had been when slipping it into the pile. Probably in the hope that Jim would be so anxious to get the job done, he would sign it without paying much attention to what it was.

On the other hand, Jim's fatal weakness had been his love for the countess. Even if Jim realized the document transferred his vast wealth to Arlette, he might have signed it anyway. How was he to know he would be dead a day later?

So now Arlette was the legal head of the Conover empire. She could do with it as she pleased. It explained why she was in such fine spirits so soon after her husband's death.

Husbands. Fargo thought of the others she'd had. Did they all suffer fates similar to Jim's? Was that why she had so many?

Voices outside brought Fargo back to the here and now. He arranged the stack as it had been, minus the document, then started toward the door. Shadows flitted toward it. He would be seen if he stepped out. Running to the drapes that shrouded a window, he ducked behind them just in time.

The door opened. In came Countess Arlette Leonie Mignon d'Arcy Conover and her male secretary. They were shoulder to shoulder, whispering and grinning. Arlette preened in a mirror while Albion went to the desk and sorted through the documents.

Fargo had pressed his back against the wall and angled his knees to either side to keep from bulging the drapes. A hand on his Colt, he watched as the albino came to the middle of the pile.

Albion flipped through another dozen. His brow knitting, he kept going until he came to the bottom. "It can't be," he said to himself.

Arlette overheard. "What can't? Is something the matter?"

"I must have missed it," Albion said. Swiftly, he flipped through the stack again, checking each and every sheet carefully. Those in the center he held up to the light, angrily throwing them onto the desk when they were not the one he sought.

"What? What?" Arlette said, coming over.

Albion did not answer until he had gone through the entire stack a second time. Leaning on the desk, his marble features showed a tinge of color for the first time. "It's not here."

"How is that possible?"

"I don't know." Albion smacked the mahogany top with an open hand. "I slipped it into the middle, exactly as you directed."

Arlette stepped around to his side. "Maybe he noticed it after all, and took it out. Check the drawers."

The desk had seven. They yanked each open and rummaged through the contents. A scowl of baffled rage contorted the countess's countenance as she straightened. "Damn it to hell! We need that transfer to establish our claim in probate court. The fool never would draw up a proper will, as I begged him to do time and again."

Albion surveyed the study. Fargo tensed when those piercing pink eyes swept past the drapes, but the albino did not detect him. In a corner stood a cabinet that Albion pointed to. "Maybe he filed it for some reason. Or stuffed it into one of his precious books."

"Or perhaps someone took it." Arlette began to pace, glowering at everything and anything, her red nails hooked like talons. "One of our wretched little servants has caught on and is trying to thwart us."

"But who?" Albion said, then tensed. "What a stupid question! Of course! It must be her! She has been snooping around ever since she arrived!"

Arlette had the look of a panther about to tear into a fawn. "I knew that she heard more than she claimed when she eavesdropped on us the other day. What a fool I was. Your warning did no good. I should have had her dealt with permanently. But I held off, thinking James would grow suspicious." Tossing her black mane, she stalked to the door. "Well, no more. Let's go pay the hussy a visit."

No sooner did the door close behind them than Fargo was across the room. Folding the document, he stuck it under his shirt. He let a minute go by before he warily stepped out. The corridor was empty.

Beverly had roosted on the edge of his bed, the toothpick at her side, the rifle clasped in trembling hands. She brightened and bounced erect when he appeared. "Thank God! I was worried sick."

"We're leaving," Fargo announced, reclaiming the Henry.

"Right this minute?"

Fargo did not reveal that the countess was out for her blood. It would only add to her anxiety, make her more of a wreck than she already was, and she needed keep her wits about her if they were to get out of there alive. "We'll head straight for the stable. If anyone tries to stop us, let me deal with them."

Beverly scooped up the knife. "I guess you know what is best. But what about all my personal effects?"

"We'll come back for them. And we'll bring a lawman along." Fargo pricked his ears for sounds of a commotion.

Once the countess discovered that the cook was not in her room or in the kitchen, a search would be launched. They had to be gone by then.

"We will?" Beverly seemed satisfied, but as they hastened from the chamber, she tugged on his arm. "Wait. What about Maline? Is it right to rush off without letting her know. Maybe she'll want to come along."

Fargo hesitated. It was true. The maid just might, after what had happened to Jim Conover. "Do you know where we can find her?"

"In her room, most likely. I'll lead the way."

As nervous as a prairie dog that knows a rattlesnake is in its burrow, Beverly guided him to the landing. The great hall lay somber and silent under a mantle of shadows. She descended rapidly, slanting to a narrow corridor Fargo had never been down before. Here she stopped short, her fingers digging into his palm. "That's strange. Usually a couple of lanterns are left lit at all times."

Total blackness was before them. It reminded Fargo of the dank tunnels under the castle, and the grisly dungeon. "How far down is it?" he whispered.

"At the far end."

Fargo assumed the lead. Leveling the Henry, he walked with the right-hand wall at his elbow. Bit by bit his eyes adjusted to where he could distinguish doorways and the niches where lanterns were supposed to be. They were gone. Someone had taken them, not merely blown them out. An ominous sign.

"There!" Beverly whispered, extending an arm.

On the right was the last door, wide open. Fargo tiptoed the final few feet. The maid's chamber was as black as the corridor. He could see the vague bulk of the bed, but that was about all. The rest of the room was an inky blur.

Beverly raised her lips to his ears. "I know where her lantern is. Give me a moment."

As tense as a fiddle string, Fargo covered her. He had not forgotten that he barely escaped from the underground levels with his life. At any second the hunchback might pounce. He was ready when the lantern flared to life, but not for the sight it revealed.

Maline Bonacieux's chamber was in a shambles. Her broken chair lay near the foot of the bed. A pile of ripped sheets and blankets was on the other side. One of the posts had been snapped clean off. Clothes were scattered about. But her dresser had not been touched, as it would have been if someone had been hunting for something. Upended on the rug was a food tray.

Beverly Shannon was the color of chalk. She gaped at the mess, her eyes misting again. "We're too late! The countess and Albion have got her!"

Fargo doubted the pair were to blame. Just a few minutes ago they had been in the study. There had not been time for them to do this. Besides, the countess was after Shannon, not Bonacieux.

"What do we do now?"

The same question nagged at Fargo. On the one hand he wanted to find Maline. On the other, every moment they lingered heightened the odds that they might not get out of Castle Conover alive. Since he could not conduct a thorough search and protect Beverly at the same time, that left him with one option. "I'm taking you out of here. I'll come back for Maline as soon as I can."

"That's not fair to—" Beverly began, recoiling when Fargo suddenly lunged and clamped a hand over her mouth.

"Shhhhh. Listen."

From up the benighted corridor came the heavy tread of a massive form, mingled with deep, raspy breaths. It grew steadily closer, steadily louder.

Damn! Fargo fumed. They were too late! He pushed Beverly around to the far side of the bed. Hunkering beside her, he rested the Henry on the mattress, aiming at the pale rectangle of the doorway at the very instant that an ebony figure filled it from jamb to jamb.

Quirinoc. It had to be. Fargo, holding his breath, waited

for the hunchback to enter. Beverly had hold of his leg and was gouging her nails in deep, as usual. He hoped to hell she would not scream and give them away.

The giant form stood there a few seconds. Then, as ponderous as an African elephant, it turned and trudged back up the corridor.

"What is he up to?" Beverly whispered.

Fargo had no idea. But with Quirinoc roaming the halls, every second they wasted might be their last. As much as he hated to leave without Maline, Beverly's safety must come first. Gripping her wrist, he hurried into the corridor.

She must have sensed his urgency because she did not speak once. Not as they ran to the main hall. Not when they sprinted to the great double doors. Nor as he hustled her across the courtyard, the cold night air biting them to the bone.

A single glowing lantern hung in the stable. The horses were restless. One pounded its hooves on the floor. Another tried to barge through the low door that penned it in.

"What's the matter with them?" Beverly wondered.

In adjoining stalls stood the Ovaro and the dun, both with their ears pricked, their nostrils flared. Fargo did not like it one bit. "Cass? Where are you?" he called out softly. "Help us saddle up."

The stable man did not answer. His quarters at the back were dark, the door closed.

"He turns in pretty early. He's probably asleep," Beverly said. "I'll go fetch him."

Fargo's saddle blanket and saddle had been draped over the stallion's stall. Losing no time, he threw them on the pinto, then hustled to the tack room for a saddle for the dun. Beverly came back, perplexed.

"Odd. He's not there. Yet his bed is turned back, as if he was about to retire. And his boots are beside it." She scratched her head. "He wouldn't leave the stable in this cold weather without his footwear. Even more peculiar, his scattergun is propped in the corner, and he never goes anywhere without it."

Call it intuition. Call it a premonition. But a stifling sensation of impending danger crept over Fargo, a feeling that unless they got out of there right that minute, they would regret it. He finished with the dun's cinch and held out a hand to Beverly. "Up you go."

Saddle leather creaked as she stepped into the stirrups. Fargo walked the stallion to the entrance and on around the corral. High up on the castle wall a darkened window frowned down on them. Even higher up reared the stark ramparts, their stone teeth jutting hungrily skyward.

Halting at the portcullis, Fargo let the reins drop. He turned to the spoked wooden wheel that worked the chain which meshed the gears and raised the gate. But the chain was missing. It wasn't looped around the wheel as it should be. Mystified, he craned his neck.

Wet drops spattered his face. A few stray snowdrops, Fargo reckoned. Then he saw the thing that hung thirty feet above his head, and his blood grew as cold as the air around him.

Cass dangled from the end of the chain. It had been looped around his neck so tight, his neck was partially severed. Like the bob on the end of a fishing line, the body rotated first to the right, then the left.

Beverly mewed like a frightened kitten. Aghast, both hands over her mouth, she exclaimed, "Why did they kill him? He didn't know about their scheme."

Fargo backed up for a better view. The chain was impossible to reach, and without it he had no means of lifting the heavy metal grill. Escape by horseback had been cut off.

As if Beverly were able to read his thoughts, she said, "Does this mean we're trapped?"

The very next second a tremendous crash rent the air—a crash so loud that the ground shook. Stone shards pelted Fargo, one lancing his scalp, drawing blood. The Ovaro reared. He had to grab the reins to prevent it from running off across the courtyard. Even so, it kicked and pulled, nearly dumping him on his knees.

Beverly cried out as the dun tried to throw her. She fought to keep it under control, but the horse wheeled into the courtyard. From out of nowhere a huge projectile crashed onto its neck, dropping the dun where it stood and throwing Beverly from the saddle.

Fargo ran to her side, hauling the Ovaro after him. Lying next to the dun was a square stone block that would have taken three men to lift. He glanced up.

Perched on the ramparts was a vision out of anyone's worst nightmare. A giant apeish figure tore madly at the battlements and ripped another heavy stone block loose. Stepping to the edge, the bestial abomination reared erect, the grotesque hump on its broad shoulders visible as it pivoted. A wolfish howl tore from its throat as, coiling forward, it hurled the block with all its prodigious might.

"On your feet!" Fargo bellowed, hauling Beverly off the flagstones. He gave her a shove that sent her stumbling toward the stable. "Run!"

His last shout was smothered by the thunderous smash of the stone block just a few yards from where he had stood. Chunks the size of apples struck him and the stallion. The Ovaro whinnied stridently. It attempted to flee, but he clung on, forcing it toward the only safe haven, the stable.

Another howl rent the night. The hunchback was tearing at the parapet in a paroxysm of primitive fury. He succeeded in freeing a third block and rose to toss it.

Springing behind the stallion, Fargo gave it a clout on the hindquarters, driving it into the stable ahead of him. A bound brought him to Beverly, still dazed and tottering. Catching her in his arms, he propelled them both through the entrance just as the third block slammed to earth on the very spot they had vacated. Rock shards battered them, but they had survived. For the moment.

Beverly leaned against him for support, sobbing quietly. Fargo stroked her hair, feeling keenly the warmth her lush body gave off and the swell of her enormous breasts against his chest. Scolding himself that now was hardly the proper time or place, he tore his thoughts from her shapely contours to the matter of staying alive.

"Quirinoc has gone insane!" she declared. "Why should he try to kill us? He hasn't hurt anyone before this!"

Fargo begged to differ, but he held his tongue. Since they were effectively trapped there for the time being, he made the best of it. "What did you mean when you mentioned a scheme?" he probed.

"I've been aware for quite some time that the countess and Albion have been up to no good," Beverly said. "Ever since I caught her slipping off into the woods with a picnic basket for a tryst."

"A picnic basket?" Fargo repeated, recalling his own encounter.

"It was last summer. I was out taking a stroll when I saw Arlette sneaking off through the trees. Naturally, I was curious, so I followed her." Beverly paused. "At the base of the mountains to the west is a small cave. Albion and she would meet there once or twice a week. Sometimes she would take food and they would stay all day."

It explained why Arlette had panicked when Fargo stumbled on her during the storm. She had been on her way to join her lover. Foiled, they had risked discovery the next day by meeting in the parlor. "Jim never caught on?"

"Usually he was off on business trips when they did it," Beverly said. "I thought about telling him. Agonized over it for weeks. But I couldn't bring his world crashing down around him. He was such a sweet innocent."

"You still haven't told me what you know of their scheme," Fargo noted.

"I'm getting to that." Beverly bowed her head, acting embarrassed to go on. "You see, quite by accident I learned that the castle is honeycombed with secret passages. Jim had no idea they existed."

"How could that be?"

"Arlette oversaw the construction. Since all she had to do was bat her eyes and he'd bend over backward for her, she begged to be put in charge. Then shooed him off to the mine so she could do as she pleased without his catching on. She must have paid the workers a lot of money to keep them quiet."

Fargo mulled her revelations. The pieces were falling into place bit by bit, but she was hiding something. Grasping her chin, he raised her face so they were eye to eye. "That was you in the passage behind my bedchamber the other night, wasn't it?"

Beverly did not respond. She had no need to. From her neck to her hairline she flushed deep scarlet. "I'm sorry," she said softly. "I didn't mean to spy on Maline and you when the two of you were . . ." She stopped, unable to go on.

"No harm was done," Fargo said, more amused then offended. In jest, he quipped, "I hope you liked what you saw."

Her flush darkened. She averted her face, though not before the suggestion of a smile curled her luscious lips.

"About that scheme?" Fargo brought it up once more.

Coughing, Beverly said, "I never knew the exact details. But the day before you showed up, I was passing the parlor and happened to hear the countess and Albion. She was laughing and saying she couldn't wait for Jim to be buried so they could be together. Albion spotted me."

"And came after you later when you were gathering wood," Fargo guessed.

Beverly nodded. "He wanted to know how much I had heard. When I wouldn't answer, he tried choking it out of me. That's when you came to my rescue." She dabbed at her eyes. "It was so frustrating. I knew they intended Jim harm, but I had no proof."

Fargo stepped to the entrance and peered up at the ramparts. Quirinoc was gone. Out in the courtyard the dun feebly kicked and twitched. Still alive, it was in extreme agony. A large jagged gash in its neck exposed shattered bone and severed arteries. One leg was crushed to a pulp. Reluctantly, he sighted down the Henry and put a mercy slug into its brain.

At the blast, Beverly gasped and ran up to him. Seeing the horse, she said simply, "Oh!" and began to weep.

Levering another .44 cartridge into the chamber, Fargo walked to his stallion. So it would not wander out into the open, he tied the reins to a post. Then he took Beverly's slim hand and moved cautiously to the corral. They crouched next to the rails, their breath forming tiny clouds.

"What are you up to?"

Fargo had made up his mind. Hiding in the stable until daylight was pointless. The hunchback or the albino would come after them eventually. By morning, if they lived that long, they would be so tired that they would be easy to pick off. There was only one thing to do. "We're going back inside."

9

The great door squeaked like a mouse caught in the jaws of a ravenous cat when Skye Fargo pushed on it. He opened it halfway and left it open in case they had to leave the castle in a hurry.

Beverly Shannon was behind him, so close that every few steps her bosom brushed his back. She had a grip on his shirt, her other hand on his shoulder. Terrified, she would be of little help if they ran into trouble. Or, rather, *when* they ran into trouble. It was inevitable. They were walking into a lion's den of madness and bloodshed.

A deathly silence gripped Castle Conover, the lull before the storm. The shadows seemed darker somehow, more menacing than ever. Each blackened corridor mouth hid a lurking monstrosity. Evil whispers and wicked titterings filled the oppressive air. It was as if they had entered the dank, foul belly of a leviathan. Doom hung on every wall, in every corner.

"I don't want to do this," Beverly said for the tenth time. She had objected bitterly out by the corral.

But Fargo was not one to cower in fear, or to wait for an enemy to come after him when he could take the fight to the enemy. Besides, it had galled him to ride off and leave Maline. With their escape cut off, he had a justified excuse for coming back in and hunting for her.

Fargo walked down the middle of the hall. Should anyone rush from either side, he could fill the attacker with lead before they reached him. He pivoted constantly, always razor alert. The wilderness had honed his instincts to a knife's edge, and he used them now as he rarely had before, to their fullest, and beyond.

If he were smart, Fargo told himself, he would come up with a plan of some kind. But for the life of him, he couldn't, beyond finding Maline and somehow getting the two women out of there. He would take each moment as it came. And pray that the hunchback was not as indestructible as he seemed to be.

Nearing the stairs, Fargo slowed. "We'll search every room on this floor first," he whispered. "Then those on the second floor."

"What about the secret passages?" Beverly asked fearfully.

"We'll save those for last. Maybe we'll get lucky and find her before that." Fargo glanced at the cook, curious how so timid a soul had found the courage to roam through the serpentine labyrinth below their feet. "How far down into the secret corridors did you go?"

"Not very far at all," Beverly admitted. "I stayed in the ones on the upper floors." She shivered at the memory. "I was too scared to go below ground."

Fargo was going to ask another question when a rustling noise whipped him around. The tapestry that hung over the corridor to the dining room was swaying. Someone—or some *thing*—had just been there. "Come on!" he declared and ran toward it, his finger curled around the Henry's trigger.

Beverly sucked in a breath, her hands clawing at his shirt so hard she would tear it from his body if she was not careful.

Footsteps pattered beyond the tapestry. Fargo shoved it aside with his rifle barrel. Down the corridor a dim shape ducked into the dining room. He gave chase, running briskly, but not at his top speed so Beverly could keep up.

In the dining room metal clanged on stone. Fargo reached the doorway and crouched, the rifle jammed to his shoulder. The chamber was empty. An upturned silver tray and a pile of food lay on the floor beside a section of the far wall that gaped black.

Fargo halted. It was another hidden entrance to the secret maze. From it blew a faint chill wind that bore with it a trace of foul odor. Now he was the one who shivered slightly as he warily moved forward.

"That's the hidden door I always used," Beverly whispered. "I saw Albion use it one day when he thought I was off working in the kitchen." She scrunched up her delicate nose. "What's that awful smell?"

"You don't want to know," Fargo said. He listened at the opening. In the distance rose maniacal laughter, too high-pitched to be either Quirinoc or Albion. It made him think of the madman who had attacked him during the storm, and the strange figure he had glimpsed from the upstairs window. His skin covered with goose bumps, he backed away.

Beverly was on her knees, examining the pile of food. "Someone helped themself to the meats we keep in cold storage and took a couple of apples from the apple barrel." She picked up a piece of ham that bore teeth marks. "I knew I was right all along."

"About what?" Fargo asked, never taking his eyes off the secret doorway.

"About food missing from our larder." Rising, she flung the ham onto the table. "Arlette insisted that I take a monthly inventory. She was a fanatic about keeping track of every item. A while back things began to turn up missing. A few canned goods, crackers and cakes, strips cut from the meat, that sort of thing."

Was it Fargo's imagination, or did he hear voices upstairs?

Beverly did not notice. She had gone on. "When I reported it to the countess, she was furious. She called a meeting of all the servants and demanded to know who was responsible. No one spoke up, so she instituted a new procedure. Everyone had to sign for their meals and snacks. Anyone caught stealing would be fired."

Fargo moved closer to the corridor. The voices had died out, apparently.

"Well, food kept on disappearing. I tried to catch the culprit, but whoever it was proved too smart for me." Beverly nudged the pile with a toe. "I know this will sound crazy, but I began to suspect that there was someone else in the castle."

Or someone who could sneak in and out at will, Fargo reflected. He had a hunch that it was one of the Utes from the original band, although why the warrior would stay in the vicinity after all his companions had been horribly tortured was a mystery. By rights, the man should have gone to his village and roused them to go on the war path against the whites responsible.

Gesturing, Fargo led Beverly into the corridor. They went from one end to the other, but found no trace of Maline Bonacieux, or anyone else, for that matter.

Twenty corridors ringed the great hall. Into each they stalked, Beverly holding a lantern over her head to light their way, his knife in her other hand. Fargo had not realized how many rooms the castle contained; there had to be a hundred. Many were seldom used, but all were lavishly furnished.

One turned out to be of special interest. They had traveled down a murky corridor near the entrance and came to a heavy iron door that bore a padlock.

"What's this?" Fargo asked.

"The Weapons Room, as the countess called it," Beverly said. "She kept it locked so none of the servants would wander in there and accidentally hurt themselves. Or so she claimed." Beverly stepped to a niche, groped along the wall, and produced a large iron key. "Maline showed this to me. She had to dust every chamber once a week, even if they were never used."

The Weapons Room was twice the size of Fargo's bedchamber. On every wall, covering every square foot of space, hung varied and exotic weapons—the kind that knights had used in medieval times. Fargo saw swords of every size and description; rapiers, poniards, double-edged broadswords, sabers, and more. There were crossbows and longbows and quivers full of arrows, long lances and broad-tipped spears, maces and battle axes, daggers and dirks.

"Quite a collection, isn't it?" Beverly said.

That was putting it mildly. Fargo roved the room. A small, light axe caught his eye. It was not quite three feet long. The head bore a wide cutting edge on one side, a shorter flanged edge on the other, and was crowned by a slender sharp tip several inches in length. Taking it down, he gave the axe a few trial swings. It was surprisingly light, easy to wield.

Beverly joined him. "What do you plan to do with that?"

"Give it to you," Fargo said. She needed something better to defend herself with than the small throwing knife. "Trade you."

Uncertainly, Beverly gave him the Arkansas toothpick and accepted the war axe. She tested it, but she was still not sure.

"If someone comes at you and you don't have room to swing," Fargo said, "poke their eyes out with the tip, or spear them where it will hurt the most."

Beverly regarded the weapon critically. "I don't know if I could. I told you before that I'm not a violent person. I've never deliberately harmed anyone."

"You'll do fine," Fargo assured her. In his travels he had met people like her who refused to bear arms no matter what. Yet when their lives were in danger, when they stood at the threshold of oblivion, more often than not self-preservation spurred them into defending themselves against their own will. Maybe the same would hold true for her. If not, well, that was her choice. All he could do was his best to protect her.

Presently, they found themselves at the foot of the wide

stairs. Fargo did not know what to make of Quirinoc's absence. One moment the hunchback was on a rampage, the next he was lying low. Why? And where were the countess the her lover? They had to have heard the crash of the massive blocks in the courtyard, yet they had not appeared. What were they up to?

Shaking his head, Fargo cautiously climbed. Repeatedly, he checked behind them. Their lives depended on being vigilant every second. Any lapse, however short, could prove fatal.

Two-thirds of the way up, Fargo suddenly stopped. To the right of the landing something had moved. He distinctly heard the stealthy pad of feet. Bending low, he hugged the rail until he was a step shy of the landing. Then, with a lithe leap, he gained the center of the corridor, hoping to take the skulker unaware.

No one was there. Fargo swung to the left. Again the empty corridor mocked him. The gloom dispersed as Beverly sidled to his side, her lantern flinging the darkness back. Elbow to elbow they moved down the right fork.

Castle Conover contained three times as many bedrooms as were needed. A few were reserved for guests. But others had never been used and likely never would be, and they were all along this corridor. Wandering their dark and gloomy confines was like wandering a ghostly landscape.

It grated on the nerves, even steel nerves like Fargo's. He tried to keep a tight rein on his imagination, but it was not easy. He saw shadowy figures where there were none. Furniture moved. He had never been so jumpy in all his life, and it angered him.

They searched two bedrooms, then came to a third. Fargo went in first, low and fast as always, hair-trigger nerves wired to explode at a hint of hostility.

Like the other bedchambers, this one contained a chair, a dresser, a four-poster bed, and a big mirror. The lantern bathed it from wall to wall. No one was there. Fargo poked his head into the empty closet, nodded at Beverly, and began to leave.

Something thumped *under* the bed.

Like a cat Fargo whirled and dropped to his knees. The bottom of the bed was only twelve inches off the floor, much too low to hide the hunchback. But not the albino. Fargo extended the Henry.

At the same moment, Beverly bent down, lowering the lantern to the carpet. Its glare washed over the petrified features of Robert Cheeves, his eyes as wide as walnuts, a hand clamped over his mouth.

"Come out of there," Fargo commanded, backing up as the butler quickly obeyed. The Englishman's balding pate glistened with sweat, and his sorrowful eyes were rabid pools of fright.

"For God's sake, don't shoot, governor! It's only me! See? I'm unarmed!" Cheeves elevated his empty hands to prove it. "I'd never harm you!"

Much to Fargo's annoyance, Beverly stepped between them and patted the butler's arm, saying kindly, "There, there. We're not going to hurt you, either. Calm down and tell us what you've been up to."

"Staying alive, miss," Cheeves said, his Cockney accent made worse by his fear. A strong scent of alcohol hung about him. "It's been horrible, just horrible! Have you seen Cass? I saw what the dreadful monster did to him."

Fargo stepped to one side so he could watch the Englishman and the doorway. "You were there?"

Cheeve's Adam's apple bobbed as he nodded. "I wish to heaven I hadn't been! Never in all my days have I witnessed such barbaric savagery! That poor Yank didn't stand a prayer. And there was nothing I could do to help him."

Beverly took the butler's hand. Seating him on the bed, she said soothingly, "Calm yourself, Robert. There's no need to talk about it if you don't want to."

"Yes, there is," Fargo disagreed.

"But you can see how upset he is. Why make him relive it?"

Fargo had to remind himself that she had never been in a situation like this; she had never had to fight for her life. She did not realize that every detail they learned might mean the difference between staying alive and winding up on the rack in the dungeon. Patiently, he replied, "The more we know, the better our chances of getting out of this alive."

Cheeves gestured. "I don't mind talking about it. Really." He ran a hand over his head, blinking forlornly. "Maybe it would even help me."

Beverly was still not happy. "Take your time," she said. "Stop whenever you want."

The butler took a breath. "Well, you know how fussy Cass was about not entering the castle? How we always had to take his meals out to him?"

Fargo interrupted. "Did he ever say why he wouldn't step foot inside?"

"I asked," Cheeves said, "but he always evaded the question, except once, when he hinted that he had seen something that scared him half to death. That's why he never went anywhere without his shotgun."

"Go on," Fargo said.

Cheeves fished under his jacket and pulled out a silver flask. Opening it, he swallowed greedily, not caring what they might think. "Blimey, I needed that," he said with a sigh. "Now where was I? Oh. Since Beverly here and darling Maline were grief stricken by the master's death, I was the one who took Cass's meal to him this evening. Everything was fine then."

Fargo frowned when the Englishman took another swallow. The man would be of no help if they were jumped.

"Later I went back for the tray and dishes," Cheeves continued. "Cass was about to turn in. We chatted a bit and he went into his room. Me, I ducked into an empty stall to nip a little brandy." He patted the flask. "The countess doesn't like for me to drink, you see, so I have to sneak it when I can."

"Was that when Quirinoc showed up?" Fargo goaded

The butler gulped. "Yes, sir. I never heard him, which was bloody strange since he moves about like a blooming rhinoceros most of the time. One second he wasn't there. The next he was. About made me wet myself, I don't mind confessing."

Beverly was as interested as Fargo now. "Did he see you?"

"I should say not!" Cheeves said. "If he had, do you think I would be sitting here right now?" He shuddered. "That awful brute moved as quietly as a tiger down the aisle to Cass's room. I had no idea he intended to harm the Yank." Another swig fortified Cheeves to go on. "Quirinoc stood to one side of Cass's door and knocked real lightly. Cass must have thought it was me. He opened the door and started to say something like, 'What are you doing back?'"

They could have heard a pin drop when the Englishman paused. Beverly licked her lips, glancing at the dark doorway.

"That terrible hunchback struck like a cobra, he did," Cheeves related. "He took hold of Cass's throat and waist and lifted him clean off the ground as if Cass weighed no more than a feather."

"Why?" Beverly asked. "What possible motive could he have had?"

"Beats me, miss," the Englishman said. "I wasn't about to ask. I was paralyzed, I'm ashamed to say. I watched as that giant shook Cass, playing with him, like. Cass tried to fight back. He was a scrapper, that one, but his punches had no more effect than if he were hitting solid rock." Cheeves started to lift the flask, but capped it instead. "Anyway, Quirinoc carried Cass outside. Somehow I got my legs under me and snuck after them."

"You should have shouted for help," Beverly said.

A haunted look came over Cheeves. "You don't know

what you're saying, miss. One peep out of me and that brute would have done to me as he did to poor Cass." He closed his eyes, "Quirinoc tore off the chain that opens the gate and wrapped it around Cass's neck. Then, as pretty as you please, he hung Cass by the neck until Cass was dead, dead, dead." Breaking off, Cheeves sank his head into his hands. "Oh, that I should have lived to see such a sight! I wish I were back in the east end of London, where I belong."

"What did you do after that?" Fargo asked.

Cheeves straightened. "I hid behind the horse trough, quaking in my shoes. Quirinoc went to the inner courtyard wall and went up it like a bloody gorilla. When I was sure he was gone, I—"

"Hold it," Fargo broke in. "Are you trying to tell us that the hunchback *climbed* the castle wall?" It was impossible. No one could scale those sheer heights.

But Cheeves nodded. "That he did, governor. And I would never have believed it if I had not seen it with my own eyes. He stuck those big fingers and toes of his in the cracks between the stones, and went up just as pretty as you please."

Fargo bent toward the bed so abruptly that the butler recoiled. "Quirinoc had his shoes off?"

"Yes, sir," Cheeves confirmed. "Don't ask me how he could walk about in the cold like he did. He's not human, that one. I mean, have you ever seen anyone who only had three toes on each foot?"

A bolt of lightning coursed through Fargo. All too vividly, he recollected the slaughter of White Eagle's band. "Three toes?" he rasped.

"I know it sounds like I'm making it up," Cheeves said. "But I swear by all that's holy! I saw his feet as clear as day, and they are as deformed as the rest of him. Each has three big toes, just like the demons in a painting I once saw. It makes me weak-kneed even to talk about it."

Fargo moved to the doorway so his expression would not

give him away to the others. The more he learned, the more worried he became.

At one time or another Fargo had tangled with some of the toughest men alive. Apaches, Comanches, rivermen, and Cajuns, callous gunmen and hardened killers; he had gone up against them all and lived to tell about it. But Quirinoc was in a class by himself. The hunchback was more beast than man, and even that did not do him justice.

Quirinoc was more like an unstoppable force of nature than a flesh and blood being. How, Fargo wondered, could he possibly protect the cook and the butler from someone so savage, so brutal, so inhuman? And as if that were not enough to keep him occupied, he had the countess and the albino and the tittering madman to deal with, too!

"Skye, are you all right?" Beverly asked.

"Fine," Fargo lied. "Let's keep looking." Palming the Colt, he held it out to the butler. "Here. Don't shoot unless you're sure of hitting what you aim at."

Cheeves smiled wryly. "I'm terribly sorry, sir, but I've never handled a firearm in my life. I'm British, you know. We like to think that we're too civilized to ever need to carry guns. Balmy, I know. But we're too set in our ways to change."

"Your choice," Fargo said, twirling the pistol into his holster. The Brit's refusal only made it harder on him, but he couldn't force Cheeves to carry one if the man didn't want to. Probably better anyway, he mused. In Cheeves's state, the butler was just as liable to shoot of one them as he was to shoot Quirinoc.

They left the chamber, Fargo in front, Cheeves carrying the lantern, Beverly Shannon holding the axe. After scouring every room on that side of the landing, they started on those on the other side.

As Fargo was about to slip into the fourth, he froze. From overhead rumbled a series of loud hammering blows. So powerful were they that when he looked up, dust settled from the ceiling onto his face.

"What on earth!" Robert Cheeves exclaimed. "Is that devilish blighter trying to bring the roof crashing down on our heads?"

"How can we get up there?" Fargo inquired.

Cheeves started. "Are you daft, governor? He would crush you like an eggshell if you dared to poke your head up."

Beverly indicated a narrow hall that branched off the corridor they were on. "Down there. A door at the end opens onto a spiral staircase."

Fargo decided to finish searching the second floor before he went up. That way, he did not have to watch their backs and be on the lookout for the hunchback at the same time. Entering the room, he was surprised to set eyes on another secret opening that yawned darkly on the left-hand wall.

It was almost as if it had been left open on purpose, as a lure. Suspicious of a trap, Fargo crept over. What he heard brought an oath to his lips.

From the chill depths below, from the haunted bowels of the earth, echoed a woman's plaintive cry. Despite the distance and the distortion, there was no mistaking the voice of Maline Bonacieux. She was wailing over and over, "Help me! Somebody! For the love of God, please help me!"

10

"That's Maline!" Beverly Shannon cried, then tried to push past the Trailsman to plunge into the secret passageway.

Snagging her arm, Skye Fargo hauled her back. "Not so fast," he warned. "It could be just what they want us to do. If we rush on down there, we could run into an ambush."

"So what?" Beverly said. "We have to help her if we can. You know that as well as I do."

She was right. Fargo did know it. But only a fool charged headlong into danger when there might be another way. So he hesitated, racking his brain. The trouble was, he could rack it forever and never come up with an alternative. They had to do it, whether he liked the notion or not.

"Well?" Beverly chafed at the delay. "What are you waiting for? Listen to her. She sounds as if she's in awful pain."

The maid's quavering voice was laced with anguish. Fargo imagined her in the grip of one of the hellish devices of torture in the dungeon. The soft creamy flesh he had molded with his hands soon might be ripped and flayed from her exquisite body. "I'll go," he said. "The two of you stay here until I get back."

"Like hell," Beverly said. "If you think you're leaving me alone, you have another thing coming."

"Quite so," Robert Cheeves threw in. "There's more strength in numbers, you know." He bobbed his chin upward. "Besides, I don't fancy being caught by that balmy monster with you gone."

Fargo had not realized the pounding overhead had stopped. Quirinoc might be on his way down. Hurrying across the chamber to the corridor, he closed the door and threw the bolt. From a niche he took an unlit lantern and used the lit one the butler carried to light the wick. "I'll go first. Cheeves, you bring up the rear. If either of you see anything, give a holler."

"Have no worry on that score," the Englishman joked wanly. "I'll yell so loud, your eardrums will burst."

Holding the lantern aloft in his left hand, Fargo entered the passage. It was narrow and dank, as they all were. The combined glow of the two lanterns lit up the inky confines for a dozen yards in both directions, which was reassuring. At least there would be some warning if they were jumped.

Fargo tried his best to recollect exactly how he had reached the dungeon the first time. But the passages all looked so much alike, and there were so many twists and junctions, that within ten minutes he was convinced they were lost. They had missed a turn somewhere. He was ready to go back when another junction stood out in stark relief before him. A chill breeze bearing a vile reek wafted from the left-hand fork. "This one," he whispered.

Neither the cook nor the butler uttered a peep. Ashen features told why. To their credit, they did not let it stop them. Fargo was most impressed by Beverly. She had stopped weeping at every little setback, and she had her fear in check. Gripping the axe securely, she was ready to cleave anything that came at them from out of the gloom.

The floor slanted gradually downward, added proof that Fargo had picked the right tunnel. The stink grew worse. Beverly coughed a lot, and soon was gagging. Stopping, Fargo removed his bandanna and offered it to her.

"What's this for?"

"Tie it over your mouth and nose to keep the smell out."

She wanted it. That was plain. But she hesitated, asking, "What about you?"

"I've come across worse," Fargo said, which was true as

far as it went. Still, after she had complied and they resumed their subterranean trek, his stomach would churn every so often, and he had to fight down rising bile.

Cheeves, a sickly shade of green, covered his nose with a hand. "Listen," he said.

The wails from below had ceased. Fargo did not like to dwell on why Maline Bonacieux might have fallen silent.

At the next junction Fargo was stumped. Here the reek was equally foul in both forks. He had no clue which one they should take. His gut instinct was to bear to the left. But something skittered across the right-hand passage at the edge of the light, so he took that one instead. Whatever it was, the creature fled, staying a few steps ahead of the glow as Fargo pushed deeper into the passage.

To catch it, Fargo broke into a run. Rounding a corner, he glimpsed something small and hairy that was gone before he could identify it. Behind him raced Beverly and Cheeves. They covered another ten yards. Fargo had just spotted another bend ahead when the tunnel resounded to a thunderous *thud* in their wake. Spinning, he raised the lantern higher. Cheeves did the same.

"God, no!" Beverly said.

An iron grill had slid down from recessed grooves in the ceiling, completely blocking off the passage. Fargo backtracked. It was pointless, but he tried to lift the grill anyway. The butler lent a hand, then Beverly. They strained until their faces were red and they puffed with each breath.

"It's no use," Cheeves said, slumping in despair. "We're trapped. They have us at their mercy now."

"We must have tripped it somehow," Beverly stated the obvious.

Fargo picked up his lantern. He blamed himself for taking the wrong turn. What other nasty surprises awaited them farther along? he wondered. "Stay close together," he advised. "From here on out we can't afford any more mistakes."

"Easier said than done, governor," Cheeves said forlornly. "I've got a bad feeling about this. A bloody bad feeling like none I've ever had."

"Shrug it off. It's just nerves." Fargo moved out, paying close attention to the walls, ceiling, and floor. Reaching the bend, he paused on hearing a strange *scritch-scritch-scritch* from the other side. Something was around there, waiting for them. Cocking the Henry, he leaped past the turn. And promptly wished he had not.

Beverly started to scream, but stifled it by clamping a palm over her mouth.

The Englishman drew back as if to flee, completely forgetting they had nowhere to run.

Beyond the rim of light blazed hundreds of tiny red eyes. They lined the floor for as far as Fargo could see. Taking another stride, he discovered a roiling phalanx of hairy bodies, twitching dark noses, and long slender tails. *Rats!* More than he could count. More than enough to eat a man alive, to strip him to the bone in minutes. So thick were they pressed that a single shot would drop tens at a time. But not even the Henry could hold back that tide of teeth and claws should the rats attack.

"Where did they all come from?" Beverly breathed. "I never saw a rat in these mountains before."

"The wharves of London are crawling with them," Cheeves said. "That's where the countess took ship for America. Her belongings were stacked on the dock for over a week, waiting for her ship to put in."

"Are you saying some gnawed into the crates and the like? That they made the trip over?"

"They do it all the time," Cheeves said. "Some vessels are notorious for being infested with the blighters." He shuddered. "Maybe only a few made it alive to the castle. But they've had a whole year to breed down here."

Fargo took a slow step to gauge the rodent army's reaction. The leading ranks edged backward, shying from the light more than from him. A large one began squeaking shrilly in alarm, and the next instant they all were chittering. A few hissed like snakes. Others bared wicked incisors and growled.

"We're dead if they come after us!" Beverly said.

"What are we to do?" Cheeves moaned. "We can't go forward and we can't go back."

"Can't we?" Fargo said, taking another measured stride. Again the tide of rats rolled back like surf fringing an ocean. He found that by lowering the lantern close to the floor and swinging it back and forth, they retreated briskly.

The chattering rose in volume as the rodents grew more and more agitated. Some crouched to leap, but they never did. Always their feral eyes were drawn to the bright radiance of the lantern, and they would retreat, whiskers bristling over spiked teeth.

Yard by yard, for minutes on end, Fargo forced the hairy horrors to retreat. They passed two bends and were nearing a third. It seemed that the deeper they went, the more rats there were. A solid wall of writhing bodies and tails surged around the corner, when suddenly a resounding crash shook the walls. On its heels rose a bedlam of high-pitched squeals and shrieks and panicked chattering.

Fargo extended the lantern past the turn. A twenty-foot-long section of the ceiling had fallen, breaking apart on impact. Huge numbers of rats had been crushed flat or had been hideously injured and were thrashing in their death throes. The rest were in full flight, a legion of rumps and tails vanishing into the gloom.

"Another trap," Beverly said.

"If not for the rodents, it would have flattened us like pancakes," Cheeves remarked.

Fargo hunkered to search the floor for some sign of the trigger that had released the massive blocks. Either it was too well concealed or it had been buried with rats. Rising, he picked a path through the rubble, careful to avoid the gnashing rapier teeth of rodents not quite dead. In a frenzy they bit at anything and everything, even one another. It was not uncommon to see a partially crushed pair, most of their limbs useless, their bodies mangled, tear into one another in berserk fury.

Beverly cried out. A rat had sunk its front teeth into the edge of the sole of her shoe. It clung on as she frantically kicked her leg.

"Hold still," Fargo said. A stroke of his rifle butt sufficed to render the rat limp. He had to grip its repulsive body to pry the teeth out, then flung it away. Wiping blood on his pants, he stepped over a pulped shape.

"I just had a terrible thought," Cheeves remarked. "What if this bloody passage is a dead end?"

Fargo had already considered that. If so, he would not give up. It was not in his nature. As hopeless as their prospects were, so long as they were alive they had a chance. "We'll cross that bridge when we come to it," he said.

Around the next turn was a long stretch of empty tunnel. Not a single rat could be seen. Fargo halted, mystified. The rodents had not had time to outdistance them, so where had all of them gotten to? He waved the lantern at the walls and floor but saw no openings.

"What's this, then, Yank?" the Englishman said, walking up next to him. "Did they vanish into thin air?" Raising his lantern, Cheeves took a few more steps. "They have to be around here somewhere. Hello! Look here!" The butler bent toward a narrow crack running lengthwise in the center of the floor. "Could this be the explanation?"

A metallic click stiffened Fargo. He saw Cheeves pull back as the floor parted down the middle, the two halves sliding under the walls on either side with incredible swiftness. Fargo lunged. His grasping fingers caught hold of the Englishman's jacket. It was the same hand that held the Henry, though, and he could not get a firm grip.

Squawking, Cheeves pitched forward. His arms windmilled, his lantern falling.

"No!" Beverly screamed, leaping to their aid. Her fingers plucked at the butler's collar, but missed.

Fargo threw himself backward, pulling the Englishman with him. For a second he thought they would make it, but the smooth material slipped through his fingers like so much butter. He lunged again, not caring if he lost his lantern or the Henry, but the harm had been done.

Robert Cheeves screeched and twisted in midair. In the glow of his falling lantern a pit was revealed, its bottom layered with row after row of gleaming metal spikes. Cheeves grasped for support that was not there, shock and fear rendering him mute at the final moment. He crashed down onto his back, the spikes shearing through him like butcher knives through a slab of beef.

Beside him landed the lantern, cracked and dented yet intact enough to show the outcome of the butler's plunge in all its gory detail.

Bloody metal points ruptured from the Englishman's body and limbs. One sliced up out of the side of his neck. Another sheared off an ear. A crimson geyser pumped from a severed leg artery, and more scarlet trickled from his nose and mouth. Incredibly, Cheeves was still alive. He gaped blankly at the ceiling, his mouth moving wordlessly.

"Robert!" Beverly screamed, leaning so far down that she slipped and fell.

This time Fargo was quick enough. Seizing her around the waist, he yanked her up next to him. Her arms went around his neck, and she held him close, quaking in misery, tears flowing freely again.

A spark of intelligence filled the Englishman's eyes. With it came searing torment. He whimpered like an infant and attempted to move, but it was hopeless. Pinned flat, he was beyond help. "Oh, God!" he said. "I don't want to die!"

No one ever did, Fargo thought grimly. Beverly's tears soaked his neck, seeping under his shirt and down his chest. He stroked her hair, helpless and hating it.

"I can't see very well!" Cheeves said. "Are both of you all right?"

"We're fine," Fargo said, a constriction in his throat making it hard to speak.

"Never bloody thought it would end like this," the butler said softly. For a while he was quiet.

Not knowing what to say, Fargo said nothing. He owed his life to the man. Had Cheeves not gone ahead, he would have stepped onto the false floor. It would have been his body lying down there, his life's blood gushing out.

The Englishman's eyes misted. "Strange what you think of at a time like this," he croaked feebly. "I remember the Thames on a sunny Sunday. Cricket matches. Guy Fawkes Day when I was a nipper." He swallowed some of his own blood and coughed. "I remember what it was like to eat fish and chips until I burst. And steak and kidney pie."

"Don't talk, Robert," Beverly said. "You'll make yourself worse."

Cheeves laughed, or tried to. But what came out was a strangled gurgle that ended in a spasm of coughing. "What difference does it make? I'm done for, lass. But it's sweet of you to care."

Beverly buried her face on Fargo's shoulder. "Won't this nightmare ever end?"

The butler's eyes closed, and his breathing grew shallow. Just when Fargo was sure the man would expire, Cheeves looked up at them, lucid for the moment.

"Sir? Would you do this old Cockney a favor?"

"If I can."

"Make those who did this to me pay for what they've done. I've always been a peaceable chap, always turned the other cheek, as it were. But I'd like to die knowing that whoever is to blame will join me in hell before too long."

"Count on it," Fargo promised.

A tranquil smile crept over the Englishman. "Bloody marvelous. Cheerio, then. I'm sorry—"

Whatever the butler was going to apologize for would remain unknown. Robert Cheeves broke into violent convulsions. The metal spikes ripped and gouged, the one in his

124

neck cutting sideways into his jugular. In moments he sagged lifeless, nerve impulses twitching his fingertips.

Fargo expected Beverly to bawl hysterically. She bent in half, about to, then clenched her fists and beat them on her thighs, saying, "No! No! Not this time!" When she looked up, fierce determination lit her face. Each new ordeal was tempering her, like steel being tempered in a blacksmith's forge.

"I want to do my part, Skye," she declared. "I want to see them suffer for what they've done to Jim and Robert."

Fargo faced the pit. Vengeance had to wait. Simply staying alive was the main chore before them. He gauged the distance to the opposite rim, judging it to be six feet, no more. "I'll go first," he said.

Beverly glanced at the bottom, then at the floor beyond. "You can't mean it. I can't possibly jump that far."

"We can't stay here," Fargo noted. Sitting, he drew the Arkansas toothpick and cut more whangs from his buckskins, trimming enough to form a long cord once he linked them with stout knots. One end of the cord went around the Henry's barrel, the other around the stock where it narrowed at the breech. Slinging the rifle over his back, he hefted the lantern, then backed up a dozen steps.

"Please," Beverly said. "I couldn't stand it if anything happened to you. I don't want to be down here alone."

Fargo concentrated on making the jump. Hunching forward, he braced his legs, curled onto the balls of his feet, and launched himself at the pit as if hurtled from a catapult. He ignored the spikes and their grisly catch; he ignored the pathetic pleading on Beverly's petrified face. Legs driving, he flew to the very brink of the cavity and at the last possible instant vaulted into the air.

It was only six feet, yet the gulf yawned like a mighty chasm. Fargo arced upward, arced downward. His outflung legs struck the rim and he dived, the weight of the lantern nearly unbalancing him. Landing on his side and shoulder, he lay still, the beating of his heart like a hammer pounding at his temples.

Beverly Shannon's delectable red lips formed a perfect *O* of astonished relief. "You did it!" she cried.

Fargo sat up and placed the lantern to one side. Unslinging his rifle, he removed the makeshift cord and leaned the Henry against the wall. "Your turn," he said, moving to the edge.

"I don't know . . ." Beverly said, unwilling to commit herself.

"Would you rather stay here until you starve to death?" Fargo did not mince words. "That is, if the rats or something else don't get you first." He wrapped one end of the cord around his left hand, the other end around his right. "Do it now or you never will."

Beverly, frowning, carefully swung the axe and tossed it across. The head clanged noisily when it hit. "Stand back," she said, backing up as he had done.

But Fargo only sidled to the left. He had a plan, a mad idea that might save her should the worst occur. Which was more than likely. She was nervous, and nervous people made mistakes. Sometimes fatal mistakes. Flexing his arms to limber them, he watched closely.

"Here goes," Beverly said. But she did not move. Fear rooted her where she stood.

"The longer you wait, the harder it will be," Fargo said, dangling the loop so that it hung close to his boots.

Beverly did not answer. Nervously rimming her mouth with her tongue, she wiped her palms on her uniform, took a deep breath, and did it. The hem of her dress swirled around her shapely legs as she sprinted toward the pit. Just as Fargo had done, she leaped out over the glittering spikes. But unlike Fargo, she did not wait until she was at the edge to jump. She hurled herself upward a few inches shy of the brink.

Maybe she would have made it if she had waited until the final moment. Maybe her terror caused her to misjudge the distance. Whatever the reason, Beverly was going to miss by several inches.

Fargo saw it at the same split second that she did. Throwing his arms behind his head, he whipped them forward. The loop of buckskin flicked out and over Beverly's shoulders just as she began to lose momentum. He timed it perfectly. The instant that the cord settled around her shoulder blades, he shot backward, digging in his heels.

His momentum, added to hers, was the extra boost Beverly needed. Her feet alighted on the rim, but she teetered and would have gone over if not for the wrench Fargo gave on the cord. She sprawled forward, her flailing hands catching hold of his shirt. Together, they fell, Fargo bearing the brunt, his arms slipping to her hips, hers around his waist.

Locked together, they lay still. Beverly was on top, cushioned by her huge breasts. Her rosy lips were so close that her warm breath fanned his cheek. "Thank you," she said huskily. "I thought I was a goner."

"My pleasure," Fargo said. Shifting, he prepared to push her off, when to his surprise she covered his mouth with hers and bestowed a lingering, passionate kiss. "What was that for?" he asked.

"For saving my life," Beverly said. Again she kissed him, this time gliding her velvet tongue between his teeth. He imitated her, aroused in spite of the circumstances. "Maline was right," she said when she broke for air.

"About what?"

Beverly responded with a smirk. Propping her hands, she began to rise. "My ma used to say that every cloud has its silver lining. Maybe she was right."

There was no need to ask what she meant. Fargo sat up, admiring the way her bosom swelled her garment.

Beverly straightened. Her gaze drifted past him. In the blink of an eye terror replaced her smirk, and she let out a bloodcurdling scream. "Look out, Skye!"

The warning came too late. Fargo shoved up off the floor and spun, but he was not quite halfway around when a heavy figure slammed into him, and fingers made of granite wrapped around his throat.

11

It was like being bowled over by a stampeding bull buffalo. The impact knocked Skye Fargo onto his back, and he felt himself slide half a dozen feet. A foot caught him in the groin. Another blow smashed into his ribs. Pain exploded throughout his body. Pinwheeling points of light danced before his eyes. A bestial face loomed before him as the man came down hard on his chest, but his vision was too blurry for him to see his attacker's features.

Fargo heard Beverly scream. He thought he heard rushing footsteps. Movement above him resulted in the pressure on his throat lessening. He could breathe again, and at the same moment his vision returned with crystal clarity.

Beverly was grappling with a disheveled figure. She had come to his rescue and was trying to pull the man off. Now his attacker had her by the wrists, and she rained a flurry of kicks.

Fargo had taken it for granted that his assailant was either Albion or Quirinoc. So he was startled to see that it was neither, and even more startled to discover who it really was. "Jasper Flint!" he blurted.

At that instant, snarling like a wild beast, Flint hurled Beverly from him. She hit the wall with jarring force and fell to her knees, dazed. Flint promptly shifted, his callused hands once again spearing for Fargo's throat.

So shocked was Fargo by the drastic change that had come over the man he knew, that he was a shade too slow in raising his own hands to protect himself. Seizing Flint's wrists, he struggled to pry them apart. "Jasper!" he said. "It's me! Skye! Don't you know me?"

A wolfish growl was the former riverman's reply. In truth, Flint resembled a wolf more than he did a man. His coal-black hair, which he had always worn neatly cropped around his ears, hung in filthy stands to his wide shoulders. His chin, always clean shaven, now bristled with an unkempt short beard as dirty as the rest of him.

Fargo remembered Flint as a dashing riverboat rogue, a fancy dresser always popular with the ladies. Now Flint's face was caked with grime, his buckskins smeared with dirt. A wild gleam of madness shone in his dilated green eyes. Yellowing teeth were bared in savage bloodlust.

Worst of all, though, was what had been done *to* him. Flint's features were a mockery of his former handsome mein. Large patches of skin had been torn off and replaced by thick scar tissue. His formerly straight nose was bent and flattened. His lips were cracked and somehow out of line with one another. His whole face, in fact, was oddly shifted, as if it had been twisted out of proportion.

As they grappled, Fargo noticed other changes. Flint's right ear was missing. One of Flint's shoulders was several inches higher than the other. His right arm seemed longer than the left. Teeth were missing, and from a hole in Flint's forehead, a hole that looked as if it had been *drilled*, oozed vile yellow pus.

"Jasper! Stop!" Fargo tried once more. They had never been the best of friends, but they had never been enemies, either. Flint had to remember the drinks they shared, the card games they played. Or did he? Not so much as a flicker of intellect was evident in the riverman's frenzied eyes.

Striving to brace his elbows under him for leverage, Fargo suddenly realized that they were on the brink of the pit. A glance showed him the rows of steel tips and the mangled body of Robert Cheeves. It lent him added strength. Shoving with all his might, he rolled to the left and drove his knee outward.

Jasper Flint was thrown against the wall. With remarkable swiftness he scrambled onto his hands and knees. Next to him was the Henry, but he made no move toward it. Hands clawed, teeth bristling, he rushed at Fargo like a creature of the deep woods, like a rabid wolf or coyote.

Fargo's Colt flashed out. He brought it up and around in a blur, the barrel striking Flint across the forehead and felling the riverman in his tracks. Pouncing, Fargo pressed a knee onto Flint's chest, grasped the front of Flint's shirt, and rammed the barrel against the wild man's cheek. "No more, Jasper! Lift a finger and you die!"

Fargo did not expect his warning to be heeded. Flint was too far gone, he figured. But amazingly, the demonic gleam faded from those blazing eyes, and the violent tension drained from the misshapen body.

Jasper Flint blinked a few times. "Fargo?" he said softly. "Is it really you?"

Nodding, Fargo slowly rose and stepped back. He did not lower the Colt, though. Beverly was rising, and he motioned for her to pick up the Henry. Together they covered the riverman as Flint sat up, grimacing. "What the hell happened to you?" Fargo demanded bluntly.

The riverman looked down at himself, his shoulders sagging, his lower lip quivering. "They did it," he said, barely above a whisper.

"Who?" Fargo said. "The countess?"

At the mention of Arlette, Flint's head snapped up and some of the insane fire flared. "Yes! That bitch! The countess and the damned albino and the hunchback!"

"Calm down, Jasper," Fargo said. "They're not here now. Neither of us will hurt you if you behave yourself."

Flint turned and acted as if he were aware of Beverly for the first time. "Howdy, ma'am," he said politely. "I hope I didn't scare you too much. I keep having these awful spells, you see . . ." His voice broke, and he raised a hand to cover his face.

Fargo winced. Three of the riverman's fingers had been broken and never mended properly. Each was bent at an unnatural angle. And the tip of his thumb was missing. "There's no need to talk about it if you don't want," he said.

When Flint lowered his hand, his eyes glistened. "No, I'd like to," he said numbly. "Someone has to know, in case something happens to me."

Still wary, Fargo stepped to the opposite wall and squatted, the Colt resting on his thigh. "Arlette Conover told me that you stopped by. She claimed that she made you leave after you insulted her."

Once more inner flames contorted Flint's face. "Is that what she says? The lying witch!" With some difficulty he regained his self-control. A lopsided grin curled his deformed lips. "You know me, Fargo. I never could resist a pretty face. Sure, maybe I was a mite pushy. But I never manhandled her. I've never mistreated any woman."

"Arlette is different from most," Fargo observed.

Flint scowled bitterly. "All I did was put a hand on her shoulder. She slapped me and told me to leave the next morning or I would be thrown out. So I went off to bed, never suspecting a thing."

Knowing Arlette, Fargo could guess what happened next. "They grabbed you in the middle of the night."

Jasper Flint nodded and cleared his throat. "Before I knew what was going on, the hunchback was dragging me down one of these passages. I tried to fight back, but he's too damn strong. Him and that albino took me to the dungeon and tied me to one of their infernal contraptions."

"It's best not to go on," Fargo said.

But Flint did not appear to hear. "The things they did to me! I don't know how long it went on. Weeks. Months. They'd torture me until I was almost dead, then force food and water down my throat and wait for me to recover enough for them to start in on me again."

"Jasper—" Fargo said.

Tears were trickling down Flint's cheeks. "Do you know what it's like to have your bones slowly broken to bits? To have skin peeled from your body strip by strip? To have your nails pulled out? The ends of your thumbs chopped off?" He groaned.

Fargo glanced at Beverly, who was horror struck.

"But those were nothing compared to what was done later," Flint went on. "I was stretched until I was sure my arms and legs would pop off. Burning coals were put on my stomach. Wooden slivers were driven into the soles of my feet."

"No more!" Beverly cried. "How could Quirinoc and Albion be so cruel?"

Flint shook his head. "You've got it wrong, missy. They switched me from one contraption to another, sure. But it was the countess who tortured me. And she loved every minute." His gaze locked on Fargo's. Sorrow and despair came over him. "She . . . she . . ." he choked off again.

"Let it be," Fargo said.

"No," Flint said, pointing lower down. "She cut them off, Skye. I begged. I pleaded. But she took a Green River knife and sliced them off, laughing while she did it."

Fargo stared at the riverman's groin, feeling sick to his stomach. No words of sympathy would suffice, so he said nothing.

"Then the hunchback stomped on them, and they held up what was left for me to see," Flint related. "That's when something snapped inside of me. I haven't been the same since."

A terrible silence fell. For the longest while none of them spoke. Fargo realized that it had been Flint he saw that night out the window. He did not want to disturb the riverman, who hugged himself and trembled as if cold. But eventually he had to, saying, "Flint, can you get us out of here? We can't go back the way we came. A heavy grill blocks the tunnel."

Jasper Flint roused. "I've been wandering these passages for ages. I know every way in and out." Rising stiffly, he shuffled toward the darkness.

Fargo was quick to grab the lantern. Beverly gave him back the rifle and scooped up the medieval axe. They followed the riverman cautiously, unsure how long the sane spell would last. No rats appeared as they wound around a series of bends. The floor angled upward by degrees. Here and there spider webs hung from the ceiling. Once Fargo saw a black widow on the wall.

"It won't be long," Flint told them.

"We're grateful for your help," Beverly said. "If you don't mind, I'd like to hear how you got away from the countess. And why you stay up here in the mountains instead of going down to the settlements."

Flint laughed, a bark of scorn. "Do you honestly think I want anyone to see me, missy? That I want anyone to know what's been done to me?" He muttered foully to himself. "As for how I got away, it's no great puzzle. Arlette grew bored after weeks of having her fun. But she didn't want me killed outright. No, that would deprive her of more pleasure later on. So she had me chained to a wall and left orders for the hunchback to keep me fed."

Fargo did not like how the riverman's voice rose in volume and became tinged with flinty spite. It would not take much to drive him over the edge again.

"My strength came back after a while, but I never let on," Flint said. "One day Quirinoc brought me a tray of food. I was pretending to be asleep. So he set the tray down and went off to do something else. But he forgot that the key ring was on the tray."

"How have you survived all this time?"

Flint glanced over a shoulder, his eyes seeming to glow with unholy glee. "I've lived off the land, girl. Whatever I can catch, I eat." he tittered. "Hard to believe, but I've grown quite fond of rat meat."

Fargo's stomach churned. He was at a loss what to do. The riverman was so far gone that Flint was beyond help. "Haven't Albion and Quirinoc tried to hunt you down?"

"Oh, they've tried, all right," Flint gloated. "But I've been too smart for the bastards." He paused. "The hunchback has come close a few times. He's a devil, that one. Stronger than a bull and faster than a sidewinder. Watch out for him, Fargo."

"I intend to." Fargo noticed that Flint had not bothered to ask why they were there, or why they were seeking to escape the castle. The man had one thing on his mind and one thing only—revenge.

"I aim to see that Arlette Conover pays for what she did to me," Flint said, confirming it. "No matter how long it takes, no matter what I have to go through, she's going to suffer just as I suffered. Before I'm done, she'll beg and plead with me just as I did with her. And I'll laugh in her face."

Another turn brought them to a short passage that ended at a solid wall. Or so it appeared. Fargo, however, felt the whisper of a cool breeze and scented the fragrance of pine.

"The countess doesn't know that I've been spying on her and her lovers," Flint said. "I know every secret door in this place."

"Did you say 'lovers'?" Beverly asked.

Nodding, Flint stopped at the wall and ran a hand over the stones near the top. "Sure did. She's like a dog in heat. Never gets enough. One night it's the albino, the next it's the hunchback."

Beverly was appalled. "She lets Quirinoc make love to her?"

Flint rose onto the tips of his toes. "You've got it backward. The countess is the one who makes love to them. She has to be in control the whole time. The whips, the ropes, they're all her idea."

"The what?" Beverly said.

"Ah, here it is," Flint declared. Pressing a spot, he stood back as a section of the wall slid open, revealing a sea of pale snow broken by islands of firs and pines. In the distance reared jagged peaks.

Fargo set the lantern down and moved into the open. They were near the northeast corner of the castle, hidden in its shadow. After the reek of the tunnels, the brisk fresh air was invigorating. He breathed deeply.

Beverly stooped to plunge a hand into the snow and run it through her fingers. "Safe at last! What do we do now?"

A grating thump behind them brought Fargo around in a flash. The hidden door had closed. No trace of it existed on the stone wall. He groped the smooth surface, seeking a knob or latch or button. There was none.

"Why did he do that?" Beverly asked. "We could help him, if only he would let us. He needs to see a doctor and get plenty of bed rest."

Fargo did not point out that it was unlikely Flint would agree to either. Rather than waste time trying to open the door, he moved westward along the wall. The windows overhead were dark, the castle quiet. So was the woodland, except for an occasional shriek of wind. They had only been outdoors a couple of minutes and already the cold was eating into his marrow. Finding shelter was essential.

"Do you have a plan?" Beverly wanted to know.

"Sort of," Fargo said. Actually, he was making do as they went along, but he did not want her more worried than she already was. Hastening to the northwest corner, he rounded it. The iron door was closed, as he anticipated, but it was also bolted on the inside, which he had not foreseen.

Beverly stamped her feet and swatted her arms against her sides. "We'll freeze to death by morning if we don't find someplace warm."

Fargo surveyed the plateau. Encased in snow and ice, the temperature well below zero, it was fit for polar bears and penguins, not humans. Where, in all that frigid vastness, could they find a haven? Inspiration dawned. "Can you find your way to that cave you mentioned?"

"The one where the countess and Albion like to meet?" Beverly nodded. "But it will take half an hour to reach it in this deep snow."

"It's better than staying in the open," Fargo said. He was anxious to have her safe and sound so he could return, somehow gain entrance, and locate Maline Bonacieux. The maid's cries had died out shortly after they entered the tunnels, and he feared the worst.

Their feet crunched through the crust. Their breath rose in smoky tendrils. The rifle became so cold that it hurt to touch the metal. He stuck his hands under his armpits to keep his fingers warm, and stomped his boots. His toes grew icy anyway, to where he could barely feel them.

Beverly fared worse. Her stride became labored, her breathing ragged. Fargo had to loop an arm around her waist to hold her up as they neared a towering cliff, its base hidden by jumbled boulders, many the size of the Ovaro. "We're almost there," she said, teeth chattering, and pointed.

Wending through the boulders, Fargo spied a black cavity. He was glad to see a sizable stack of dead branches beside it. Albion, he guessed, liked to keep plenty of firewood on hand.

Eager to get in out of the cold, Fargo hustled Beverly into the cave. The place smelled of smoke from previous fires. It extended ten feet, then bore to the right.

Beverly sagged against Fargo. He half carried her around the corner, and with her in his arms, he could not do a thing when a tall pale figure materialized in front of him, holding a leveled pistol.

"What a pleasant surprise," Albion said drolly. "And here we weren't expecting guests."

The cave ended in an oval chamber ten feet wide by six feet long. Against the right wall a tiny fire sputtered. Blankets had been spread out beside it, and rising from under them, her features crinkled in wicked mirth, was Countess Arlette Leonie Mignon d'Arcy Conover. "You were right, lover," she told the albino. "You did hear voices."

Beverly had stiffened and was elevating the axe. "You! Here!" she bawled.

A flick of a wrist, and Albion relieved her of her weapon. The revolver he had trained on Fargo did not waver. "Where else would we be, idiot, with that stinking hunchback on the rampage?"

"Now, now," Arlette scolded. A heavy fur coat, a wool sweater, and fur-trimmed pants kept her nice and warm. "Is that any way to talk about dear, lovable Quirinoc?"

"Lovable, my ass!" Albion groused. "He's a raving lunatic. We should have disposed of him long ago." He shoved Beverly against the wall, then took the Henry and the Colt from Fargo.

Held at gunpoint, there was nothing Fargo could do other than let the albino do as he wanted. His guns were laid on the blankets. Albion gestured for him to back up several steps, and after he obeyed, Albion let the pistol droop a hair. "What are we going to do with them?"

"I haven't decided yet," Arlette said, planting herself in front of Beverly. Cupping Beverly's chin, she snapped, "See what your snooping has got you?"

Beverly swatted the countess's arm. "You have your gall, witch! I'm not the one who murdered Jim!"

Arlette snickered and winked at Fargo. "Listen to this hussy. She acts so damn innocent and pure. But she lusted after Jim from the day she met him. She wanted him all to herself. And she was furious when Jim came back from Europe married to me."

"That's not true!" Beverly cried, but her tone and her expression made a liar of her.

Arlette was enjoying herself. "Did you think I didn't know you were always sneaking around the castle, spying on me? You pathetic wretch."

Unexpectedly, Beverly slapped the countess. Stupefied,

Arlette pressed a hand to her red cheek, then delivered a precise punch to the jaw that staggered Beverly. Arlette would have hit her again, but the albino grabbed her wrist.

"Enough of this petty bickering," Albion broke in. "What are we going to do with these two? We certainly can't let them live. They know too much."

Arlette, fuming, lowered her arm. "So what? They have no proof that Utes didn't kill my husband."

Fargo finally spoke. "We don't need any. Every lawman in the territory is going to know that the Utes weren't to blame."

"What are you talking about?" Albion said. "Why wouldn't they believe that Conover was hacked to pieces by Ute tomahawks?"

"For the same reason I didn't," Fargo said. "You told me that all the warriors in the war party carried one. But Utes are more partial to knives for close infighting and butcher work."

Arlette shrugged. "So we made a small mistake. Tribes back East use tomahawks all the time. How were we to know it was different out here?" She regarded Beverly venomously. "Now we'll just claim that the Utes used knives to kill poor Jim. Just as they used knives to kill the two of you." With that, she walked to a leather pack, rummaged inside, and pulled out a big Green River knife.

Fargo remembered what Jasper Flint had told him. He saw her jerk the knife from its sheath, saw dry stains on the blade, and his blood boiled.

Beverly had straightened. "You'll never get away with this, Countess," she said.

Giddy mirth tinkled from Arlette. "Always the fool, aren't you, my dear? I'll have you know that I've been getting away with it for over fifteen years. I had five husbands before your precious Jim, and each met his end in an untimely manner."

"Why?" Beverly asked.

"It should be obvious, even to a simpleton like you. For

the *money*." Arlette advanced, wagging the knife. "I need a lot to live in the grand style I prefer."

"But Jim loved you!"

"So did the others. I happen to love Albion. That made them liabilities."

"And what about Quirinoc? Do you love him, as well?"

"You know about him? Well, so be it. The only reason I made love to that dolt was to keep him in line. Everything went just fine until he caught Albion and me together yesterday. We had to get out of the castle or he would have killed us." Arlette playfully slashed at Beverly's neck, narrowly missing. "Enough chitchat. I can't wait to slit your throat from ear to ear!"

12

Skye Fargo did not like staring into the barrel of a cocked
pistol. At any moment Albion might see fit to squeeze the
trigger. His every impulse was to jump the albino before it
was too late. But it would be suicide unless he could dis-
tract Albion first. Then the women did it for him.

Beverly Shannon recoiled as Arlette Conover came at
her again. The Green River knife flicked like the darting
tongue of a snake, almost taking out Beverly's left eye. She
retreated and Arlette pressed in, the lust to kill stamped on
her twisted features.

Albion made a mistake. Instead of keeping his eyes on
Fargo, he glanced at the women, smirking like the devil he
was at the prospect of the countess drawing blood.

Fargo tensed, but waited, balanced on the balls of his
feet. He would have one chance and one chance only, so he
must not slip up.

"What's the matter, hussy?" Arlette taunted. "You're not
afraid, are you?" A cut aimed at Beverly's stomach was a
fraction short. "Can it be that you're a coward at heart?"
Another playful slice was directed at Beverly's ribs.

Albion gestured. "Quit toying with her and get it over
with. We still have the frontiersman here to deal with."

"As you wish, lover," Arlette said, then sprang in
earnest, spearing the Green River knife at Beverly's thigh.
Beverly sidestepped, but not swiftly enough. The keen edge
sheared into her uniform and on into her leg, drawing
blood.

Arlette tossed back her head and howled with glee. Albion laughed, too. And Beverly, flushing beet red, did the last thing either of them ever expected her to do; like an enraged tigress she threw herself at the countess. Caught off-guard, Arlette tried to bring the knife to bear, but Beverly wrapped a hand around her wrist, another around her throat, and drove her backward. Hissing and snarling, a pair of she-cats, they struggled fiercely.

Albion took a step toward them.

It was the chance Fargo needed. Leaping, he batted the revolver aside. It went off, thunderously loud in the confines of the cave. Then he did just as Beverly had done, locking a hand on the albino's wrist and the other around Albion's throat. Chest to chest, they strained and heaved and danced every which way, neither able to gain an advantage.

Fargo lost track of Beverly. She was on her own. There was nothing he could do for her until he took care of Albion, and the albino was doing his utmost to thwart him. For so lean a man, Albion possessed whipcord muscles of steel. They were more than evenly matched. Albion might even be a little stronger.

Suddenly, they collided with a wall. Fargo's shoulder lanced with pain, but he grit his teeth and fought on. Albion was trying to point the revolver at his midsection. He was attempting to keep it from leveling. Swirling and huffing, they spun to the right. Neither had an idea where they were in relation to anything else. But they found out. For when they stopped, panting, their veins bulging, Albion squawked in alarm.

They were beside the fire. The albino's right foot was in the flames, and his soft European-style shoes with their thin soles offered no protection. He jerked the leg up, losing his footing when Fargo pushed. Grappling savagely, they fell. Albion's right arm was jarred, hard. The pistol skittered across the stone floor.

Losing his weapon drove Albion into a frenzy. He

snapped a knee at Fargo's groin, striking Fargo's leg instead when Fargo shifted. Wrenching his left arm free, he slammed a punch against Fargo's head and drew back his arm to do it again.

Fargo landed a blow of his own, a crisp cross to the jaw that rocked the albino backward. Separated, they scrambled to their knees, then traded more punches, Albion fighting with a practiced precision that showed he had some experience at boxing. Each of his blows was aimed where it would hurt the most.

Blocking and countering, Fargo gave as good as he got until he misjudged an uppercut that left him wide open. A sledgehammer smashed into his jaw. He wound up on his back, his arms flung outward.

Albion, sneering, thrust his right hand under his coat and swept it out holding a dagger with a golden hilt. Hiking the dagger overhead, he lunged, thirsting to make the kill.

Fargo's right hand had brushed something on the floor, something long and thin like a broom handle. Realizing what it was, he had curled his hand around the haft, and now he swung the battle axe just as the albino pounced.

The blade sheared into Albion's knife arm at the elbow, chopping it clean off. Blood spurted, and Albion shrieked. The stump flapping like a broken wing, he began to rise.

In a twinkling Fargo was erect. The axe clasped in both hands, he swung it once more, with all the power in his shoulders behind the swing.

Albion looked up. He opened his mouth to scream, but he never did. The axe sliced through his neck as if it were so much soft clay. Albion's head toppled to one side, the body to another.

"Nooooooooooooooooo!"

The anguished cry reverberated off the walls like the death wail of a banshee. Fargo started to turn and was shoved by a figure flying past him. He reached out, but missed. Arlette Conover, screeching madly at the top of her lungs, fled on around the corner and out of the cave. Fargo went to go after her, then saw Beverly on her hands and knees. He rushed over.

"Are you hurt?"

"Just winded," Beverly said, straightening. Blood stained her wounded thigh and her upper left arm. She had a few small cuts on her face, one on her neck. "It was close. She nearly had me."

Fargo boosted her to her feet. He saw her glance at the albino, then blanch. "Don't move. I'll be right back."

It did not take long to drag the body outside and toss the head next to it. Gathering an armful of wood, he added enough to the fire to flood the cave with light and warmth. He used a strip cut from a blanket to mop up the blood as best he could, then made Beverly sit so he could doctor her wounds. "We'll need bandages," he said, bending to slice a length of material from the hem of her uniform."

"Do what you have to," Beverly said wearily.

A water skin was beside the pack. Pouring some into a tin cup, Fargo cleaned the wounds on her neck and arm. They were shallow, no threat to her life. He dipped the cloth in the cup and nodded at her leg. "That, too."

Rather shyly, Beverly raised her dress up past the cut. The sight of her creamy thigh made it difficult for Fargo to concentrate. The wound was slight and had already stopped bleeding, but he bandaged it anyway. He could not help brushing his fingers against the inside of her leg, and each time he did, she gave a tiny shiver. "Sorry," he said.

"You've nothing to be sorry for," Beverly said huskily.

Fargo tossed the bloody water in the cup outside. He saw no sign of the countess, although deep in the forest a twig snapped loudly. He doubted she would come back. Even so, he took the precaution of rolling enough fair-sized boulders into the mouth of the cave to form a barrier. They would not keep anyone out, but someone climbing over them was bound to make noise.

Fatigued and cold, Fargo rejoined Beverly. She had found a coffeepot, and the fragrant aroma of brewing coffee made Fargo's mouth water. As he took a seat, she smiled and showed him a tin filled with eggs and strips of bacon.

"We won't go hungry, at any rate. They stored enough here to feed two people for a week. You rest, and I'll fix us a meal."

Fargo was not about to argue. He was famished and sore and had a throbbing welt on his head where the albino had struck him. While Beverly smeared butter on the bottom of a frying pan and set to work, he busied himself checking and cleaning the Henry and the Colt. Come daylight, he would need both in prime working order.

Beverly hummed to herself, the happiest he had seen her since they met, despite their predicament. Every so often she would cast coy glances his way.

It figured, Fargo mused. Women had an uncanny knack for picking the most awkward times and places to wax romantic. Yet they liked to claim that it was the men who didn't know any better.

The coffee was done first. Fargo gratefully accepted a steaming cup and slowly sipped. It was delicious, piping hot and strong enough to melt a horseshoe. Between the fire and the coffee, he was warm clean through in no time.

Beverly ladled four juicy strips of bacon and the same number of eggs onto a plate. She sprinkled salt and pepper on the eggs, then handed the plate to him with an air of expectancy, as if it were supremely important that he enjoyed what she had cooked.

A savory mouthful sufficed to convince Fargo that she could do wonders with the most basic ingredients. "Tasty as can be," he complimented her, and received a warm peck on the cheek.

They ate in silence. Outside, the wind moaned every few minutes, and each time Beverly stiffened and glanced anxiously at the bend leading to the cave mouth.

"You can relax," Fargo said after the fifth instance. "Arlette is not about to come back. She'll probably sneak into the castle."

"With Quirinoc on the rampage?" Beverly said skeptically.

Fargo downed more coffee, then smacked his lips. "Where else can she go?" he responded. "She can't stay out in this cold air very long. She'd freeze to death." He shook his head. "No, she'll hide somewhere in Castle Conover. It's her only hope."

"I wish Quirinoc would do to her what he did to Cass," Beverly said bitterly. "It's the least she deserves. The woman is unspeakably evil." She paused. "I wonder if she knows that Jasper Flint is in there, too? He would gladly rip her to pieces."

"I hope he's in his right mind if I run into him tomorrow," Fargo said, lifting the cup.

Beverly gripped his arm. "What? Don't tell me that you're planning to go back in there yourself?"

"Have you forgotten about Maline?" Fargo asked. She released him, and polished off the coffee in several great gulps.

"You're taking me with you," Beverly said.

"No."

"I won't stay here all by myself. Arlette was right. I'm not ashamed to admit that I'm scared to death. I don't want to let you out of my sight."

"We'll see," was all the commitment Fargo would make. Leaning back, he fluffed a folded blanket that served as a pillow, then lay on his back. The combination of the hot meal and the fire had him feeling as drowsy as a hibernating bear. He yawned, then shook himself to try and stay awake.

Beverly set down her plate and stretched out on her side beside him. "I can never thank you enough for saving my life," she said softly, putting a hand on his chest. "But I'd like to try."

"What did you have in mind?" Fargo asked with a poker face. As if he could not guess.

Her cherry lips lowered and dallied in a light kiss made

more tantalizing by flicks of the silken tip of her tongue. Her huge breasts bulged, and her right leg slid over his. "Mmmmm," she said when she parted. "Your kisses are marvelous. Maline was right."

"What did she tell you?" Fargo wondered.

"That of all the men she has been with, you were the absolute best," Beverly said. Her cheeks turned crimson. "And after what I saw when the two of you were together, I'd have to agree." With that she kissed him again, only this time greedily, hungrily, as if to eat him alive, her mouth mashing his, her hands roaming over his torso and up into his hair.

Fargo had to be careful where he touched. Avoiding her cuts, he stroked her cheek, her neck, her shoulder. When his right hand dipped to her breast and slipped under her uniform to cup her hardening nipple, Beverly cooed and squirmed and panted in blatant lust.

"I want you so much," she said.

Fargo didn't doubt it. Her hands were everywhere, tugging at his shirt, at his pants. Her shyness, apparently, was only skin deep. Once aroused, she was a hellion. Each kiss had more fire than the last. Each moment she grew bolder. It mildly surprised him when she pressed a hand over his rising member and stroked up and down. His own passion ignited, he looped an arm around her back and ground her against him.

Her breasts were magnificent. Swelling larger than any he had ever seen, they spilled from her uniform when he undid the buttons. Sliding lower, he licked a path from her chin to the cleft between them. She was sensitive there and wriggled sensuously. At the first contact of his mouth with a nipple, she arched her spine and dug her nails into his shoulders.

"Oh! Oh! Yes! Like that!"

Tweaking the tit, Fargo gently eased her onto her back. Her legs parted, but he did not explore their treasures just yet. Covering both mounds, he squeezed and molded them until she was pulling on his hair and thrusting her hips up against him.

Transported by rapture, Beverly licked her full lips and moaned. She glued a hand to the back of his head, entwined her fingers, and pressed. Fargo took as much of her breast into his mouth as he could, lathering it with his tongue. Beverly accidentally brushed the sore knot. He flinched, but did not stop what he was doing.

Nothing short of a cave-in could have persuaded him to stop now. Whether it was a result of the ordeal they had been through, or her ample charms, he craved release as much as she did.

While Fargo fanned her carnal desire, he stripped her naked. It was warm enough in the cave that she would be comfortable. In fact, it was so warm that Fargo broke into a sweat and separated to take off his own clothes. Habit dictated that he place his gun belt within quick reach, the butt of the Colt toward him.

"Ohhhh, my," Beverly husked, running her hands over the rippling muscles on his back and sides. "There isn't an ounce of flab on you."

Fargo could have told her why. Wilderness life was a hard life. She would call it grueling. It bred hardiness in those who called it home. In order to survive, they had to be as tough as the land. Packing on extra pounds was a civilized luxury few could afford.

Smothering a breast with his mouth, Fargo continued to arouse her. His hands roved over her flat belly to the bushy triangle below, and from there down into the nether warmth of her inner thighs. He avoided the bandage, caressing the skin around it. Her legs hooked behind him, pulling him closer. It was plain what she wanted, but he was not ready yet.

Beverly bent her head to his shoulder to nip his skin with the tip of her teeth. She leaned over an ear, her hot breath fanning his neck. Her tongue glided to his lobe. Closing her mouth on it, she sucked and nibbled.

A shiver of delight coursed down Fargo's backbone. Switching to her other breast, he gave it the same treatment as the first. Her thighs rubbed his. Her nails delicately pricked his arms and his ribs.

Suddenly, Beverly's hand swooped to his pole. A gasp escaped him. She knew just what to do to bring a man to the boiling point, and she did it, slowly, languidly, relishing the sensation as much as he did.

One good turn deserved another, Fargo reckoned, slipping his hand between her pillowy legs to the soft down that framed her womanhood. She breathed deeply and clutched at him, her eyelids fluttering in abandon. When his forefinger brushed her moist slit, she bucked against him, opened her legs wider, and tried to insert his organ.

Fargo inserted his forefinger instead. Beverly groaned, then rained hot kisses on his neck and chest. His first stroke elicited a stifled outcry. His next brought her up off the blanket, a thrashing whirlwind of desire unleashed. Her hands were everywhere. Their mouths met and locked. In due course he replaced his forefinger with his manhood.

"Ahhhhh! Yesssss!" Beverly sighed, carnal tremors rocking her. "Do it to me, big man! Do it!"

"Whatever you say," Fargo responded, then thrust into her to the hilt. It nearly lifted her off the floor. Her thighs clamped tight. She met each thrust with a counterthrust, the friction building until their molten cores bubbled, on the verge of exploding.

"I'm almost there!" Beverly cried, throwing her head back and clutching the blanket under them for added leverage. "More! More!"

Holding her hips with both hands, Fargo pounded into her. He did not hold back. She heaved against him, matching stroke for stroke. Faster and faster they went. Harder and harder they pumped.

"Nowwwww!" Beverly exclaimed, gushing. So did Fargo. Her limbs wrapped tight around him. They plunged and swayed and went over the brink together. The cave seemed to heave under them. Then Fargo had the illusion of drifting down from a great height, as light as a feather, to come to rest nestled on her heaving globes and stomach.

For the longest while neither moved. Fargo drifted in and out of sleep, the crackle of the fire a lullaby in his ears. She fell asleep, too, her rhythmic breathing adding to his lassitude.

It must have been past midnight when Fargo found the energy to sit up and dress. Beverly slumbered on, and he did not wake her. Both of them were in bad need of a good night's sleep. Adding enough fuel to the fire to last for hours, he covered her with the blankets, then crawled under them with her.

In moments Fargo was sound asleep again. His last thought was that he should get up in the middle of the night to throw some more branches on the fire. But he overslept. The flames were down to tiny red fingers when he opened his eyes.

A chill had crept into the cave. Rising quietly so as not to disturb Beverly, Fargo soon had the fire roaring again. Strapping on his gun belt, he walked to the opening. Pink fringed the far horizon and a few birds were signing. Dawn was not far off.

Fargo collected more firewood and carried it inside. It was enough to last until noon. If he wasn't back by then, he never would be, and she would have to fend for herself. Beverly stirred when he set down the wood, but she did not wake up.

Next, Fargo refilled the coffeepot and placed it on a flat stone close to the fire. The aroma would bring her around after a while, after he was long gone.

Fargo picked up the Henry. It had more stopping power than the Colt, so it made more sense for him to take the rifle and leave the pistol. But what if Beverly had need of a gun while he was gone? Quietly, he put the Henry in front of her curled form, close to her hands. It would be the first thing she saw when she woke up.

149

Having done all he could, Fargo departed. He slid over the barrier, crept through the boulders, and paused where the deep snow commenced. Arlette Conover's tracks were as plain as the dawning day. He followed them off into the trees, her stride showing that she had fled in a panic. No doubt she had figured that he would give chase.

Several hundred yards from the cave, the countess had slowed to a walk. Her erratic wandering hinted that she had been uncertain of her next step. Or perhaps Albion's death had been more of a jolt than Fargo gave her credit for. Maybe, just maybe, she had truly cared for the albino.

For a while Arlette had sat on a log, pondering. She had grown cold, testified to by a patch of stomped snow. At last she had risen and headed eastward, as Fargo had known she would.

The trail led straight to the rise. From dense cover Fargo scanned the castle. There was no sign of life. He was about to move into the open and spring to the west wall when a massive shape heaved into gigantic silhouette on the frigid battlements.

It was Quirinoc. Shirtless and shoeless, the hunchback wrapped his brawny hands around a pair of merlons for support and leaned far out to scour the woodland to the west. Even at that distance, Fargo could see the giant's bulging sinews. Layer after layer of knotted muscle covered every square inch of the deformed killer's chest and arms.

Who was he looking for? Fargo reflected. The countess?

Scowling, the hunchback drew back and shambled to the north corner of the ramparts. Again he surveyed the countryside. Angrily, he smacked the stone, then moved eastward. Evidently, he was making a circuit of the castle.

The moment Quirinoc was out of sight, Fargo broke from cover. Arlette's track led to the iron door at the northwest corner. The night before, that door had been bolted on the inside. Now it hung partway open. Did the countess have a secret means of opening it? Or had someone left the iron portal hanging wide on purpose, to lure them in?

Snow was drifting into the corridor, white wisps spreading with each gust of wind.

Pausing in the doorway, Fargo drew his Colt. Usually he did not keep a cartridge under the hammer, but in this case he made an exception and loaded all six chambers. Cocking it, he squared his shoulders, pulled his hat brim low, and stalked into Castle Conover.

The time had come for the final showdown.

13

Skye Fargo advanced down the shadowy corridor, every nerve on a razor's edge. His ears were pricked for the faintest sounds. Other than the moan of the wind through the open door, the same sinister quiet shrouded the castle. He passed a lit lantern, but he left it in its niche. This time he was not going to advertise his presence. Supreme stealth was called for if he was to have any hope of saving Maline and dealing with the hunchback.

At the junction Fargo turned right. He had been this way before and knew the direct route to the great hall. As silently as the Sioux who had taught him the art of the silent stalk, he passed one darkened doorway after another. Whispers stirred the air, whispers he blamed on the wayward wind.

Presently, Fargo spied a rectangle of pale light ahead. That had to be the great hall. Low sobs brought him to a halt. When no other sounds were heard, he moved on in a pantherish crouch.

Near the end of the corridor Fargo pressed his back to the left-hand wall and sidled the last few feet. Nothing much had changed. The cavernous hall reared stark and dim, shadows dancing in the flickering glow of the few lanterns that ringed it.

Fifty feet from the bottom of the stairs a new lantern had been placed on the floor. No one had left it there by accident. In its light huddled a pathetic whimpering figure who had been staked out as bait, much as sheepherders in the old country would stake out one of their flock to lure marauding wolves into their rifle sights.

Maline Bonacieux was a portrait of misery. Her black dress had been torn and was caked with dust and filth. Her disheveled hair hung as limply as her shoulders. Racking sobs tore from her anguished soul. Visible on her right cheek was a nasty bruise. Her temple bore a welt the size of Fargo's thumb. Tears shone on her cheeks when she looked around in abject despair at her surroundings. She shifted, and something rattled.

Fargo's eyes narrowed. A spike had been pounded into the floor. A short length of chain linked it to a shackle around her ankle. Only someone with enormous strength could have driven that stake in. Only Quirinoc.

The hunchback was not the fool the countess believed him to be. It was a clever trap. No one could free Maline without making noise that would bring the monster on the run.

Yet Fargo never hesitated. Dashing out, he ran to the maid's side. She gaped at him in astonishment, so dumbstruck that she did not utter a word until he was on his knees, examining the shackle. Then she cried, "*Monsieur! Non!* You must flee! Your life is in great danger!"

"Quiet!" Fargo commanded. But the damage had been done. Her yell echoed up the stairs. No normal man could have heard it from up on the castle roof, but within moments a loud thump resounded far overhead, the thump of a door being slammed.

"*Mon Dieu!*" Maline said.

Fargo holstered his pistol, drew the toothpick, and bent over the shackle. He had picked a few locks before, but he was not very skilled at it. Inserting the tip into the keyhole, he worked the blade back and forth, prying at the tumblers. They refused to give.

"Hurry, please!" the maid pleaded.

Added incentive came from on high. A tremendous roar rent Castle Conover, just such a roar as a giant with no tongue might make, a hideous undulation, like the roar of a grizzly and the howl of a wolf and the yip of a coyote all combined into one. It lifted the short hairs at the nape of Fargo's neck and made his palms clammy.

Maline whimpered. "Oh, he is coming! He is coming!"

Fargo twisted the toothpick sharply, not caring if he damaged it. He had to get her out of there before Quirinoc descended. Anxiously, he picked at a tiny inner lever, felt it give, and exerted pressure on the next. Sweat broke out on his brow. The roar had faded to an unnerving silence that was somehow more menacing. His mouth was as dry as sand.

"Faster! Faster!" Maline begged.

Fargo was doing the best he could. Another tumbler gave and he wedged the knife in deeper. The shackle was European-made, unlike any he had ever seen. He'd heard that master locksmiths could make locks no one could pick, and he fervently hoped this was not one of them. A click encouraged him. But still the lock did not open. In frustration he wrenched the blade to the right, then to the left.

The shackle popped apart.

Fargo did not waste a precious second. Grabbing Maline's arm, he rose and hauled her erect. "Can you walk?" he asked, seeing her legs quake.

"I think so," Maline said, leaning on his arm for support. Her gaze strayed past him. Terror widened her eyes and choked off her breath. She did not say what she saw. She did not have to.

The Trailsman whirled. On the lower landing towered an inky bulk rendered more monstrous by its misshapen profile. The hunchback moved into the pale light, his single eye a gray gleam of fiery hate, his huge fists clenching and unclenching, the three large toes on each foot curled around the edge of the landing.

Maline staggered backward. "No! Stay away!" She tried to flee, but her legs buckled, pitching her onto her hands and knees. "Help me!" she wailed. "We must run!"

Fleeing would be pointless. Fargo knew they would not get twenty feet before the hunchback caught them. But he would be damned if he was going to just stand there and wait to be killed. Shoving the toothpick into Maline's hand, he drew the Colt, hoisted her upright, and headed for the great doors at the far end.

Maline was so weak from fear she could hardly stand. Fargo held her close as he backpedaled, never taking his eyes off Quirinoc.

In three incredible bounds the hunchback vaulted from the landing to the floor. Raising one huge arm over his head, he thumped his barrel chest and let out with another fierce roar. Fargo took it as a prelude to an attack, but Quirinoc merely shambled slowly forward, stopping when he came to the stake and chain. Inspecting the shackle, the brute scratched his head, as if he could not figure out how Fargo had freed his captive without a key.

Fargo lengthened his strides. If only they could reach the courtyard! The chain clanked when Quirinoc dropped it, and the hunchback turned toward them. In a burst of speed that belied his size, Quirinoc darted in pursuit, halting abruptly when Fargo extended the Colt. For a full ten seconds the hunchback stood there, motionless. Then he hurtled at them again, only to stop a second time when Fargo took deliberate aim.

"He is afraid of your gun!" Maline declared.

Maybe, Fargo mused. Maybe not. The devious churnings of Quirinoc's mind were impossible to fathom. Perhaps the hunchback had an ulterior motive for playing cat and mouse with them. Whatever the reason, half a dozen times Quirinoc charged, and half a dozen times he drew up short when Fargo extended his revolver.

"Why do you not shoot him anyway?" the maid urged.

Fargo wanted nothing more than to fill the monster with lead. But Quirinoc was being crafty, never coming closer than fifty or sixty feet. At that range Fargo could not be sure of bringing the giant down with the first shot, and if he failed to, the wound might provoke Quirinoc into attacking. Fargo would rather wait until they were out in the bright sunlight.

The great doors beckoned. One was ajar. Shimmering rays of sunshine streamed through. Somewhere a horse nickered. Another answered.

"Look!" Maline said.

Quirinoc was angling to the left. He wore a ghastly, mocking smile, as if he knew something that they did not. Loping to a tunnel as black as the bottom of a well, he disappeared into its depths.

Maline shuddered. "What is he up to now?"

Fargo would have given anything to know. Reaching the entrance, he ushered the blonde out into the welcome glare of daylight. A few horses milled at one end of the courtyard. The dead one was stiff and cold, a solitary fly buzzing about its ruptured neck. Giving it a wide berth for Maline's sake, he entered the stable.

The Ovaro was still tied to the post. Thanks to bales of hay stacked nearby, it had been able to satisfy its hunger. But it had not had a drop to drink since Fargo left, so he promptly untied the reins and led it to a trough.

Maline, keeping watch, said, "Now all we have to do is saddle a horse for me, and *voilà!* We are gone!"

"It won't be that easy," Fargo said. She was not aware of what had happened to Cass, or the closed portcullis. "Stay here." He started to go back out, but she stuck a leg in front of him.

"Where are you going?" she asked apprehensively. "Surely, you will not leave me all by myself!"

"You're safer in here than out there," Fargo said. "I have to try and open the gate." Patting her shoulder, he took another step, then snapped his fingers at a sudden recollection. Pivoting, he jogged to the rear of the stable, to the small room Cass had lived in. Propped in the corner was the stable man's scattergun, right where Beverly had said it would be. Breaking it open, he verified both barrels were loaded and hurried out.

Maline was peering nervously into the courtyard. "I thought I heard something."

Fargo gave her the scattergun. "This will stop even Quirinoc. Use both barrels, one right after the other. Aim for his head or his chest."

Timidly, Maline accepted the weapon. "I have never killed anyone, *monsieur*," she said. "In truth, I have never so much as harmed a fly."

"It's either you or him," Fargo said. Pecking her forehead, he slipped past. He was loathe to leave her alone, but it was better than taking her into the courtyard. For all he knew, the hunchback was up on the roof, waiting to rain more massive blocks down. Colt in hand, he glided to the corral.

Nothing moved. No hulking figure filled the doorway to the great hall. No one appeared on the battlements. Why, then, did Fargo feel that hostile eyes spied on him? The rails at his back, he skirted the pen, avoiding a shattered block from Quirinoc's previous rampage.

The portcullis was still down. Fargo glanced up at the spot where Cass had been hanging and was startled to find the stable man gone. Puzzled, he looked around. Cass's body was lying at the bottom of the east wall, in shadow. For a moment he thought that someone must have lowered it to the ground. Then he saw the severed head and realized that the chain had ripped through what was let of Cass's mangled neck.

But where was the *chain*? Fargo asked himself, turning toward the mechanism that raised the gate. It was there, sure enough, dangling near the spoked wheel. Quickly, he grabbed the bottom links and pulled. Without the wheel to add leverage, raising the immensely heavy portcullis taxed him to the limit. But he refused to give up. Inch by inch, he raised it until the bottom was six feet in the air. A little further, and they could ride out.

Suddenly, a shrill scream shattered the courtyard. "Skye! Look out!" Maline yelled.

Fargo had no time to secure the chain. Looping it once around the wheel, he spun and brought up the Colt. By then Quirinoc was almost on top of him. Instantly, he fanned the revolver three times. At each blast the hunchback was jolted, but Quirinoc kept on coming.

A runaway steam engine plowed into Fargo. Iron arms encircled him, and he was lifted bodily into the air. The hunchback's snarling face was inches from his. Spittle flecked Quirinoc's thick lips. Madness gleamed in his frenzied eye.

Fargo tried to use the Colt again. But the hunchback hurled him as easily as he might throw a rag doll. The world turned upside down. With an impact that jarred every bone in his body, Fargo was dashed against the wall. The Colt fell from his limp fingers. Stunned, he could barely think straight.

"Skye!" Maline called.

Fargo was in no shape to respond. He struggled to sit up as a human mammoth loomed in front of his blurred eyes. Fingers as thick as railroad spikes hooked into his shirt. Again he was lifted, again he was thrown.

Fargo hit on his right shoulder close to the portcullis. Searing pain swamped him. His right arm went numb. Pushing up with his left hand, he saw Quirinoc lumbering toward him. The hunchback took his time, smirking smugly, confident in his power. No man could long stand up to him and live. Trading blows, fighting fair, would only get Fargo killed. And Fargo had no hankering to die.

Quirinoc reared over him. Pretending to wrap his hands around an imaginary throat, Quirinoc squeezed and twisted, showing what he was about to do to Fargo. His smirk widening, he bent. His hands extended.

The hunchback's single eye was fixed on Fargo in vicious triumph. Fargo recoiled as if he were afraid. At the last moment, as Quirinoc's fingers were about to close on his neck, he lashed out with his good arm, driving two rigid fingers into that unblinking orb.

Quirinoc snapped erect. Covering his eye, he howled. He did not see his quarry roll behind him.

Cocking both legs, Fargo slammed them into the hunchback's legs below the knees. Taken by surprise, Quirinoc sprawled forward. Scrambling after him, Fargo lunged, wrapping his left arm around the giant's ankles. It was like trying to upend two tree trunks, but he did it. With a desperate heave, he tripped Quirinoc and brought the hunchback crashing down.

Feeling began to return to Fargo's right arm as he shoved off the ground and darted to the spoked wheel. Grasping the chain, he freed it, and paused.

Quirinoc was on his stomach. Grunting, he rolled over, blinking his eye to clear it. It never seemed to occur to him that he was in any danger. Then he saw Fargo. He glanced at the chain just as Fargo let go. Understanding lit his watery eye, and he looked up. He was directly under the portcullis.

The hunchback tried to save himself. He thrust both muscular arms up to catch the ponderous gate as it fell. But not even his immense strength could stop the portcullis from smashing onto his chest. The tapered tips of the vertical bars sheared into him. It was the same as being impaled by six butcher knives at once.

Quirinoc perished without another peep, without so much as a twitch. His great head sank back, red foam flecked his lips, and he was gone.

Fargo staggered to his Colt. His ribs were on fire, and he had a hunch one or two were cracked. He turned to discover Maline a few yards away, gaping at the hunchback.

"You did it!" she breathed. "I did not think it possible!"

Just then a harpy's cackle rose from the castle's ramparts. Both Fargo and Maline craned their necks. Perched on the battlements was the countess, and she was beside herself with glee. "I can't thank you enough!" she taunted. "With him out of the way, I can do as I please. Since you have no proof that I've committed a crime, I'm free to take control of Jim's empire! I'm rich again. Rich! Rich! Rich!"

Behind Arlette gleaming steel flashed. She rocked on her heels as her chest burst open. Over two feet of a curved sword transfixed her. Clutching it, she shrieked, and was shoved over the precipice. Tumbling end over end, she crashed to the courtyard to lie in a disjointed broken heap.

Another figure took her place on the battlements. Jasper Flint's hair whipped in the wind as he howled like a coyote and danced a jig. "At last! The witch is dead!"

Fargo moved in front of Maline to block her view of the shattered remains of her former mistress. To Flint he shouted, "Come on down, Jasper! It's over. You've had your revenge."

Flint stopped prancing. Sadness claimed him. Stepping to the edge, he called down, "It's not quite over yet, my friend." He held his arms out from his sides as would a swimmer about to take a dive, then did just that, neatly and cleanly sailing out from the rampart.

"No!" Fargo hollered.

Maline screamed.

It was a flawless dive. Wearing a strange smile, Jasper Flint landed beside the woman who had driven him over the brink, his crumpled body folding in on itself like an accordion.

Fargo steered Maline toward the stable. They would saddle up, load a pack horse, fetch Beverly, and get out of there before another hour went by. The law could handle the rest.

Maline felt the same way. "I can't wait to leave! Once we reach Georgetown, I'm going to treat myself to a hot bath and crawl into bed for a week."

Skye Fargo mustered a grin. "Want some company?"

LOOKING FORWARD!
The following is the opening
section from the next novel in the exciting
Trailsman series from Signet:

**THE TRAILSMAN #185
BULLET HOLE CLAIMS**

*1860, the raw, rough, wild land
where the new states of Iowa and Minnesota touched.
This story is based on real events, proving that
where there are no laws, even good men turn bad . . .*

Fargo cursed under his breath as he pulled his muscled body out of the lake. It was such a serene, beautiful spot that he'd let himself forget the single most important rule in this wild, fierce land. He had let his guard down. He had let the beauty of place and moment dull his usual sense of caution. He had slept at the edge of the lake, and when the warm sun of morning came he'd slipped into the refreshing water, swam and washed the trail dust from his body and reveled in the moment. And now, as he stepped almost naked, wearing only b.v.d.'s, he saw six figures waiting for him, figures he would have heard, smelled, or sensed had he been alert.

No Yankton Sioux, no Iowa, Oto, or Osage, he saw, but he could feel no relief at that as he took in the six men with hoods over their heads, only their eyes visible. Skye Fargo's own eyes flicked to the holster and the Colt lying beside his bedroll, and he silently cursed again, the gun beyond reaching in one, quick dive. He looked at the hooded figures and knew that his near nakedness was not simply a matter of outer garments. The men dismounted, all except one, who stayed on his horse and kept a heavy buffalo rifle trained on him. Fargo edged closer to the Colt. "That's far enough," a man in a blue-checked shirt said from within his burlap hood.

"What are you doing in these parts, mister?" another man asked.

"Passing through. It's a free country," Fargo answered.

"Not good enough," the man in the blue-checked shirt answered.

"Going to meet somebody," Fargo said and edged his foot forward.

"We know that," the hooded figure said.

"You do?" Fargo frowned.

"Don't play dumb with us, mister. We know why you're here," the figure said.

Fargo frowned at the hooded figures. "You boys are making some kind of mistake," he said and slid another foot forward.

"You made the mistake, mister, and now we're going to teach you a lesson," the man said. Fargo saw the five figures holster their guns as they started to move toward him. That left only the man in the saddle with a gun out, and he had a bad angle, Fargo saw. Gathering the muscles in his calves and thighs, Fargo rose on the balls of his feet, let the five men come a step closer, until they all but obscured the rifleman's sight line. Twisting his body as he went into action, Fargo flung himself forward in a low dive for the Colt.

He felt a bullet graze his shoulder as he hit the ground, and then a blow came down on the back of his neck. He tried to close his hand around the Colt, had felt the leather of the holster when another blow smashed into his head. He rolled, took another smashing blow atop his head, felt sharp pain, and then a gray curtain coming down over his eyes. He shook his head and the curtain half parted. He shook his head again, saw the ground against his face, felt the dampness of it, and then he was being lifted to his feet. The last of the grayness dissipated, and he became aware of ropes around his wrists just as his face slammed against the bark of a peachleaf willow. He felt his arms pulled forward, tied around the trunk of the willow, his face and chest pressed tight to the tree as more ropes tied his legs to the tree. He could turn his head enough to see the hooded men in a half circle around the tree.

One man wearing a heavy silver belt buckle held a long horsewhip in his hands. "Go ahead, teach him about coming this way again," another voice said. The man's arm came up, and Fargo felt the whip lash across his naked back. A half cry, half oath fell from his lips as the whip bit into his flesh, a sharp, cutting pain that was instantly followed by another lash.

"Give it to him," another voice urged, and the whip lashed across Fargo's back again, the pain a sharp, intense sensation. It was only the beginning, an introduction to a kind of pain he had never experienced before.

"Bastards. What's this all about, damn you?" he called out.

"You know, mister, and you won't be forgetting," the voice answered through its hood.

"You're right about that," Fargo returned and winced as the whip descended across his back, and he felt his flesh quiver with the blow. The man wielding the whip bent to his task with a sadist's pleasure. The lashes whipped into Fargo's back, each bringing a red welt, some opening the skin in long strips. Fargo gritted his teeth with each lash, and the level of pain shot upward with each new blow until pain became the only sensation in the world. Almost the only one. Rage and fury still churned through him as his back became a raw, burning expanse. And still the lashes descended. But the crack of the whip was growing fainter. Not because the blows were weakening but because waves of dizziness assaulted him and Fargo felt himself growing weak. The whip curled around his shoulders, then moved down to the back of his legs to open new areas of searing pain.

The agony grew worse. He was consumed by pain, and it seemed his entire body was afire and still the whip found new places to land. The men's voices were only dull, unintelligible sounds now, and only the raging anger inside Fargo kept him from losing consciousness. But finally he felt his body sag, and then, dimly, he was aware they were cutting him down. He felt himself collapse on the ground, his body being turned onto his raw, burning back, and he managed to cry out in protest. But the whip came again, across his chest and then, in a final explosion of excruciating pain, across his groin. He knew he was trying to draw his legs up as the whipping stopped. He tried to cling to consciousness, but the overwhelming pain defeated even his willpower and he felt the world slip away, grayness, then blackness descending over him.

He had no idea how long he lay there, or even if he was still alive. He existed in a void, suspended in a sphere without sense or feeling. He was dead, so far as he knew, without consciousness. But then there was something, a flickering of sensation. It began not with suddenness, not with an explosion of feeling but with a tiny, creeping awareness. Wetness, first. He felt wetness. Thought wriggled through his dimness. The dead didn't feel wetness. The dead didn't feel anything. The good news pushed through the void, and he would have cheered had he been able to do so. He was alive and wondered if he heard the sound of trumpets. The wetness came again, against his face, soothing and gentle. It was a ridiculously difficult effort for him to pull his eyes open, Fargo noted, but he did so. The world began to take form again, shapes coming into focus, a blade of grass, a small stone, a piece of wood. He saw the shapes through one eye as his cheekbone lay against the earth. The cool, gentle wetness came again, across his forehead. He started to lift his head and heard his cry as his entire body seemed to explode in pain. "Oh, Jesus," he screamed and dropped his face back onto the ground.

He heard the voice, then, gentle and full of sympathy. "Easy, easy . . . slowly, very slowly," it said, a sweet, soft voice.

"Oh, God," he groaned as he slowly turned his head as the pain swept over him. He blinked, let the figure come slowly into focus, as if materializing out of a fog. He saw long blond hair appear, framing a face with a straight, thin nose, light blue eyes, and pale pink lips that formed a wide mouth, a small face that held a wan kind of loveliness. "Who—who are you?" he muttered.

"That's not important. Helping you is important," she said, and he saw the wet cloth in her hand. "Do you think you can ride?" she asked.

"I'll ride, no matter what," he said. He started to pick himself up and heard his own shout. "Oh, Jesus . . . Jesus," he groaned as his entire body erupted in pain, his back afire. But she was beside him, holding him by one arm, helping him to stand. "Oh, God, Jesus . . . damn them, god-damn them," he groaned as he forced himself to stand and felt the agonizing pain. He swayed, glad for her hand supporting him.

"Don't move," she said and swam from his sight as a wave of pain swept over him. He fought away dizziness, and when his vision returned she was beside him with the Ovaro. "I'll help you up," she said. He cursed in agony as he pulled himself onto the horse, bent forward in the saddle, and fought off the pain. When he was able to straighten up, he saw her on a short-legged dun-colored mare, holding the Ovaro's reins in one hand. "Hang onto the horn," she said as she slowly moved the horses forward.

Excruciating pain shot through Fargo with every step the Ovaro took, but he clung to the saddle horn with both hands and groaned curses. The young woman led the way to the other side of the lake, fading in and out of his sight as he fought off waves of pain. The journey seemed to take days and he tried to keep his eyes on the long blond hair only a few feet from him.

"Where?" he gasped out.

"A line cabin. Trappers often use it in bad weather," she said and kept the Ovaro at a slow walk alongside her mare. Finally, Fargo looked up and saw a sturdy cabin set back from the water. She was at his side as he slid from the saddle, held his arm as she led him into the cabin, where he saw a single room, neatly tended. She walked him to the cot against one wall. "I think you'd best lie on your stomach," she said. "That's not as raw as the rest of you."

He lowered himself onto the cot and cursed in pain as his groin came against the sheet. "Don't move. I'll get a bucket of water," she said. "I've got to clean the blood away." He lay unmoving, listened to her leave and return. He felt her pull away the remaining strands of his shredded b.v.d.'s and ever so gently used a wet cloth on his back and legs. Though his skin automatically winced at her every touch, the cool water brought some small measure of relief. Finally, when she stopped, he heard the dismay in her voice. "It's all so terribly raw. I'll go try to find something better than water," she said.

"In my saddlebag, a small bottle, leather covering on it," he said and lay still as she hurried from the cabin to return with the little plug-stoppered bottle. She opened it, poured a little onto her hands, and began to gently apply the salve to the raw skin of his back. He felt the soothing instantly take effect and groaned in gratitude.

"What is it?" the young woman asked.

"Balm of gilead, wintergreen compress, hyssop, and a touch of lard for thickening," Fargo said. "Best salve for cuts and bruises you'll ever find." He fell silent as her hands moved up and down his back and legs. She had a good touch, and his eyes were only half open when she spoke again.

"Can you turn on your side?" she asked.

"Guess so," he said. He used the power in his arms and shoulders to shift onto his side, and she began to apply the ointment to the welts across his groin. She began to apply the salve, and he felt her slow, hesitate, and then her fingers touching, lifting where one of the lashes had curled around his organ. Finally she stopped, and he lay onto his stomach again. "Thank you," he said. "Angels have names, don't they?"

"Abby," she said softly. "Abby Hall." She stepped back, and for the first time he was able to see her fully without waves of pain clouding his vision. He saw a slender, almost wraith-like figure in a blue dress, a figure entirely in keeping with the wan loveliness of her face, narrow-hipped and narrow-waisted, small breasts that were completely right on the slender shape. Yet for all her smallish, shy figure fashioned of modest, almost adolescent dimensions, she had a very contained, adult calm that gave her the incongruous quality of a sensuous wood nymph.

"Thank you, again, Abby Hall," Fargo said and winced as he moved on the cot.

"You get some sleep," Abby Hall said. "Let the ointment do its work."

"Sleep," he echoed. "Now, that's a real good idea."

"I'll be back tomorrow. You stay right there till I come,"

the young woman said. "I've put your gun and holster beside the cot, though I'm sure you won't be needing them."

He nodded, and it was no effort to let sleep come to him the moment she disappeared from the cabin. He fell into a deep sleep. There'd be time to sort out what had happened when the burning, searing pain lessened and let other thoughts take charge.

He slept heavily, despite the pain at his every move, and woke after morning had come to the sound of a horse stopping outside. He reached down with one arm, felt along the floor and found the holster and the Colt, had the gun in hand as he lay stomach down on the couch. The cabin door opened, and with a sigh of relief he saw the slender shape and the long blond hair.

She wore the same blue dress and carried a small basket in one hand. He lowered the gun, let it drop to the floor as he watched her come to the cot. The long blond hair had been freshly brushed and hung loose and full around her small, wan face. Again he had to note the strange incongruity of her, an odd admixture of shyness and sensuousness. "Hello, Skye Fargo," she said, and his eyebrows lifted.

"How do you know my name?" he asked.

"A letter addressed to you in your saddlebag," Abby said, her wide mouth suddenly smiling. "Nothing mysterious," she added, her eyes moving to his back. "How do you feel?" she asked.

"Better but lousy," he grunted.

Her gaze stayed on his back. "It'll take a lot more healing, but that salve has done wonders. I'll put on some more," she said. He put his head down as she took the bottle and poured out more of the salve. He felt her hands gently massaging the ointment into the welts and still raw skin. The ointment soothed, but so did her touch, he realized, long, soft strokes that combined delicacy and firmness.

When she had him turn on his side to salve his groin, her touch was less hesitant, he noted, yet just as lingering, and he watched her face as she applied the ointment to his organ, saw her lips part, her eyes taking in the strength of him, her hand staying, on the edge of caressing before she pulled back suddenly, as though she were afraid of her own thoughts.

He smiled inwardly as he lay back onto his stomach and watched her close the ointment bottle. "It's nice to have your own angel of mercy," he said. "You're very good at this. Practice or natural talent?"

"Not practice," she said quickly. "I've never done anything like this before."

"Never put salve on anybody?"

"Never touched a man like this, all over, I mean, naked and all," she said, and he heard the embarrassment in her voice.

"Somehow, I don't think you mind." He looked at her and saw a pink flush come into her face as she looked away.

"You'll be needing more tomorrow," she said.

"Will you come back to do it?" he asked. She didn't look at him as she nodded, the pink still suffusing her face.

"I've food for you in the basket," she said.

"You can't stay?" he asked.

"No, not today. I'll stay longer tomorrow," Abby said.

"How did you happen to find me?" Fargo asked.

"I was riding by just before it was over. I stayed in the trees. There was nothing I could do," she said.

"Just luck, then, for me," Fargo said, and she nodded.

"I had to try to help you after they left," she said.

It was an answer that left a lot unanswered, but Fargo decided not to press further. He watched her as she let her eyes move over him again before she started to walk from the cabin. She walked with a careless kind of grace, narrow hips swaying rather than swinging, breasts hardly moving at all. He lay still and listened to her ride away as thoughts danced through his mind, pulling together little pieces of what had happened. His attackers could have killed him, but they hadn't. That said something right there. They'd let him stay alive for only one reason: so he could tell others what had happened to him.

But who and why? he asked himself. They had mistaken him for someone else. Whom did they want him to warn? The questions simmered, and he cursed the men who had whipped him within an inch of his life. He wanted to pay them back and have them answer the questions that hung inside him. But was it possible to track them down, and was it worth the time and effort? he wondered. He had commitments to meet and places to be. His thoughts went to Abby Hall. Had she really happened by in a stroke of luck? It was possible, yet he had a built-in skepticism about that kind of luck. Or did she know those who had whipped him so mercilessly? Had shame as well as mercy played a part in her helping him? The question didn't make him any less grateful to her, but it hung in his mind as he went to sleep again, the body making its own demands.

He woke when the night was deep, investigated the contents of the basket, and found cold chicken. He listened to the distant call of timber wolves as he ate. He slept afterward until day came, woke with the skin of his back feeling a lot less raw.

Abby arrived a few hours later with another basket, clothed in a deep green skirt and shirt that, against the blond hair, made her resemble the gracefulness of an evening primrose. "How is it this morning, Fargo?" she asked.

"Better," he said.

She quickly began to apply the ointment to his back, but he felt a difference in her touch, her fingers moving with longer, slower strokes, almost caressingly where his back had begun to heal. When she came to his groin, her pale pink lips parted again as she made a special effort to concentrate on her task. She had just finished salving the strong, soft-firmness of his organ when he reached up and closed his hand around her wrist. "Stop . . . sit a minute," he said, and she lowered herself to the edge of the cot as he lay on his stomach. "Tell me about Abby Hall. Where does she go when she leaves me?" he asked.

"Home," Abby said.

He brushed back a lock of the long blond hair and decided there was a definite loveliness to the small face, its wan quality deceptive, masking a quiet strength. "You've family there?" he questioned.

"Ma and Pa and two brothers. We have a hog farm, mostly polands," she said, leaning back. He saw the smallish breasts nonetheless made sweetly definite points in the shirt.

"Tell me, do you know the men who attacked me?" he queried.

"No," she said quickly, too quickly. He smiled inwardly. "Why would I know that?" she asked.

"You can't live too far away. I wondered if you recognized any of them," Fargo said mildly. She shook her head but didn't look at him, he noted. "They mistook me for somebody else. You have any idea who it might have been, or why they did?" he continued, and again she shook her head. Fargo decided not to press her further as he saw the tightness touch her wide mouth. The subject bothered her, he saw. Abby knew more than she was telling, and it upset her. He'd wait to see if she'd come to volunteer more, he decided and put his head down. Finally she finished and stood up.

"I'll be back in the morning," she said. "Don't forget to eat tonight. It's important to keep your strength up." She gave him a smile, the first she'd given, and there was an almost bashful sweetness in it. She paused at the door. "That beautiful horse of yours has been grazing nearby," she said and hurried on. He listened to her leave and settled down on the cot, felt sleep eager to fling itself over him. When he woke, the night was deep, but he could feel the healed skin on his back, the burning almost completely gone. He swung from the cot, stood up, and carefully stretched. There were still areas of his back that hurt, and he took slow steps to the cabin door and gazed out. The moon traced a silver path across the lake, and the black and white form of the Ovaro quickly appeared and came to the cabin door. He stroked the horse's snout and neck.

"Soon, old friend, soon," he muttered and retreated into the cabin, where he was not unhappy to sink down on the cot again. He slept at once, and when morning came he woke, moved, stretched, and felt how much the night's sleep had helped. Abby arrived soon with another basket, paused, and glanced down at the one on the floor.

"You didn't eat," she said reproachfully.

"Slept through. I'll eat later," he said. She was wearing the blue dress again, and the fabric clung to her breasts as she sat on the cot and started to rub in the ointment.

"You are healing quickly. I think in another day you'll be able to put on clothes," she said.

He picked up something in her voice. "You sound disappointed." He smiled, waiting, but she didn't answer. "Am I wrong?" he pressed, his voice gentle.

Her voice was almost too soft to hear, and she gave a tiny shrug. "No," she breathed and he saw her look away. "That's terrible of me, isn't it?" she murmured.

"Which? Feeling that way or admitting it?" he asked.

"Both," she said, a thoughtful furrow touching her smooth brow.

"No, you're just being honest with yourself, and that's

always good. Not enough of us are," Fargo said and saw the light blue eyes studying his face.

"I've never done this before," she said.

"Tended to anyone?"

"Touched a man all over, massaged a man," she said.

"Never?"

"A few boys, a little touching, but nothing really. And now, with you, it's all so different," she said. "I'm feeling things I never felt before." She stopped, and a rush of pink flooded her face. "I didn't mean that the way it sounded."

"It's brought out caring, nursing, tenderness, all the wonderful feminine things that are part of you," Fargo said.

"What about the other things I'm feeling?"

"Desire? Wanting? They're as much a part of you as caring and tenderness. They're wonderful, too," he said.

Her eyes stayed on him. "Why here with you? Why are these feelings happening to me now?" she asked.

"Some things make their own time to happen," Fargo said.

"It's like I don't know who I am anymore," Abby said.

"It's called discovering yourself. It can be upsetting," he said as she began to rub ointment into his back.

"Indeed," she said softly, and he felt the long, slow caressing of her fingers. Finally, when she finished, she rose at once. "I must go," she said, hurrying to the door, head turned away as if she didn't dare look at him again. He stayed on the cot after she rode away, dozing off. He finally rose, went to the door, and watched the day turn to dusk. He stretched, felt the marked improvement in his back, and ate the delicious spiced rabbit in Abby's basket. He found himself thinking more about her than the men who had whipped him. She had pushed them aside in his thoughts, become her own mystery, a beautifully wan sprite, the strange mixture of shyness and sensualness in her growing stronger with each passing day.

Finally, he returned to the cot, stretched out, and turned thoughts to the note that had brought him, still in his saddlebag. It had been a long time since he had heard from Ben Brewster, and the letter had brought back a time past he'd never forgotten. He'd never liked Brewster terribly much, but that wasn't important. He was indebted to Brewster, and that was more important than liking the man. And so he had come to answer the letter, a plea he very much wanted to answer, a debt he wanted to pay. He had wondered about being called here. It was not Ben Brewster's kind of land. It was a land too powerful, too raw, too new. In some places it was called Iowa, in others, Minnesota. But the land knew nothing of man's arbitrary divisions.

His borders were only marks on a map. The land knew only itself, fertile, rugged, rich in timber and soil and wildlife. The law had long ignored this land, leaving it to pioneers, adventurers, and the red man. It had been left for those to do on their own as best they could. He stretched again, liked the way his body felt, and went to sleep with a small, wan, and quietly lovely face in his thoughts. When morning came, he rose and felt almost his old self. He rose, went outside and called the Ovaro to him, took a pair of b.v.d.s from his saddlebag, and pulled them on. He was sitting on the edge of the cot when Abby arrived. Her eyes widened as she saw him. "Surprise," he said.

Her little smile held a touch of ruefulness. "Not really," she said.

"I waited for you before going down to the lake. I'd like to wash away all the dried ointment," Fargo said.

She stepped around him, her eyes scanning his back. "Yes, you're almost all healed."

"Come with me," he said, rising and taking her hand. She gave a shrug as she walked at his side. "You know, it really hasn't been fair," he said as they halted at the water's edge. "My being naked as a jaybird all these days and you being all proper and covered."

She regarded him thoughtfully as he stepped into the lake. "That was the way of it," she said carefully.

"I know," he said from waist deep in the water. "But you could change that."

"Why?" she asked evenly, not returning his smile.

"Because you want to," he said.

The tiny, thoughtful furrow he had come to know touched her brow, and she said nothing for a long moment. Then, without a word, her arms rose, and with one motion she lifted the dress and half slip beneath it, flinging both garments on the ground. He heard the quick, sharp intake of his breath as he stared at her. She seemed a wood nymph that had stepped beautifully and unself-consciously naked out of the forest, a vision where less was more and more was unneeded. He saw a new boldness to her as she stood motionless, chin lifted upward, enjoying his enjoyment of her.

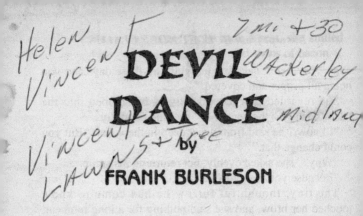

DEVIL DANCE
by
FRANK BURLESON

The year 1858 dawns blood-red in the untamed Southwest, even as in the East the country moves toward civil war. Leadership of the most warlike Apache tribe has passed to the great warrior chief Cochise, who burns to avenge the poisoning of an Indian child. Meanwhile, the U.S. Army is out to end Apache power with terror instead of treaties.

As these two great fighting forces circle for the kill on a map stained by massacre and ambush, former dragoon officer Nathanial Barrington finds no escape from the clash of cultures he sought to flee. He is drawn west again to be tempted by a love as forbidden as it is irresistible—and to be torn between the military that formed him as a fighting man, and the hold the Apaches have on his heart and soul. . . .

Prices slightly higher in Canada   (18731-8—$5.99)